光盘安装步骤

1.打开光盘,点击setup.exe进行安装。

2.点击"下一步"开始安装。

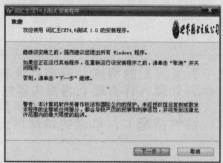

3.同意条款,并选择"下一步"继续安装。

4.可以不输入内容,按默认配置,选择"下一步"继续安装。

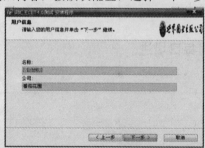

5.按默认配置,选择"下一步"继续安装。

6.按默认配置,或更改安装路径,选择"下一步"继续安装。

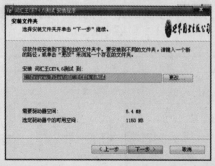

单词按难度和使用频度划分为基础、拓展、提高和飞跃四个级别。

根据历年考试中有关词汇的测试，有重点地将考点进行分析，单词处理有详有略；考点内容包括：衍生词，同反义词，近义词辨析，常考的固定搭配（短语搭配、结构搭配），单词的特殊用法。

按天计划，单词每日增进。

黑框中的词汇为历年考试的常考词汇，记忆时多注意。

使用说明

基础词汇

push
/puʃ/

vt. **推动;逼迫**
She pushed herself to her feet.
她费劲地站了起来。
短语　push... aside 把……搁置一边

drive
/draiv/

v. **推动,发动**
The urge to survive drives them on.
求生的欲望驱使他们继续努力。
搭配　drive at 朝……努力

pain
/pein/

n. **痛苦**
A cut gives pain.
割伤引起疼痛。
辨析　pain 疼痛,苦痛
　　　hurt 伤害
　　　sore 痛处,溃疡
短语　at pains 尽心,费尽苦心

call
/kɔːl/

n. & v. **喊叫;打电话**
Will you please call me a taxi?
请你给我叫一辆出租汽车好吗?
同 summon
短语　call on 拜访

拓展词汇

swift
/swift/

adj. **快的,敏捷的**
The river is too swift to swim.
这河水流太急,不能游泳。
同 speedy
反 slow

awake
/ə'weik/

v. & adj. **醒着的;叫醒**
We awake next morning to a fine drizzle.
第二天早晨我们醒来时天在下着蒙蒙细雨。

but for

要不是
But for the doctor's skill, he would have died.
要不是医生医术高明,他早就死了。

Week③Day④

7.默认配置，选择"下一步"继续安装。

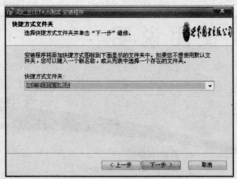

8.按默认配置，选择"下一步"继续安装。

9.安装完成，点击"完成"，并根据信息提示，选择是否立刻重启计算机。

10.安装完成，点击"完成"，退出安装程序。

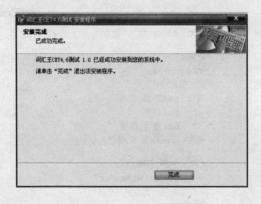

测试说明

本词汇测试程序收录了大量的测试题，题目与书中的词条对应，按单元划分，可以按单元进行测试。另外，每10个单元，安排有阶段测试，对已学习的部分进行反复训练。每次测试，程序自动从相应题库中抽取10道题进行测试，测试者点击相应选项进行测试，测试结束后，程序会自动呈现测试结果。另外，每次测试限定时间为15分钟，测试者可以根据界面右上角的时间提示掌握做题速度。

题型说明

所有测试题为选择题，题型为：

- Alternative Word　根据题目里括号中的词在上下文中的意义进行选择
- Fill-in-blank　根据上下文填空
- Definition Match　寻找相应的英文释义
- Synonym Encounter 寻找同义词
- Antonym Encounter 寻找反义词

Vocabulary

CET4,6

词汇王

赵霞 编

Vocabulary Master

世界图书出版公司

西安 北京 上海 广州

图书在版编目(CIP)数据

词汇王 CET4,6/赵霞编.—西安:世界图书出版西安公司,
2008.3
ISBN 978 - 7 - 5062 - 9401 - 0

Ⅰ.词… Ⅱ.赵… Ⅲ.英语—词汇—高等学校—水平考
试—自学参考资料 Ⅳ.H313

中国版本图书馆 CIP 数据核字(2008)第 034131 号

词汇王 CET4,6

编　　者	赵　霞
责任编辑	杨　英
视觉设计	吉人设计

出版发行	世界图书出版西安公司
地　　址	西安市北大街85号
邮　　编	710003
电　　话	029 - 87214941　87233647(市场营销部)
	029 - 87232980(总编室)
传　　真	029 - 87279675
经　　销	全国各地新华书店、外文书店
印　　刷	西安建筑科技大学印刷厂
开　　本	880×1230　1/32
印　　张	9.375
字　　数	360 千字

版　　次	2008 年 3 月第 1 版　2008 年 3 月第 1 次印刷
书　　号	ISBN 978 - 7 - 5062 - 9401 - 0
定　　价	22.00 元

目　录

UNIT 1

基础词汇

label
/'leibl/

n. 标签；商标

Put labels on your luggage.
在你的行李上贴上标签。

同 brand

搭配 label...as（尤指不公正地）把……归类为

quantity
/'kwɔntiti/

n. 量，数量

This is a question of quantity, not quality.
这是个数量问题，而不是质量问题。

同 amount, volume

radical
/'rædikəl/

adj. 根本的，基本的；激进的

This is a radical error.
这是一个根本性的错误。

衍 radicalize *v.*

同 drastic

vacant
/'veikənt/

adj. 空白的；神情茫然的；空闲的

There is a vacant post in the company.
公司有一个空缺的职位。

衍 vacancy *n.*

同 devoid, unoccupied

反 full, occupied

zone
/'zəun/

v.& n. 使分成地带，分成区；地区

The city was zoned for factories and residences.
城市被划分为工厂区和住宅区。

短语 zone time 当地时间

基础词汇

ability
/ə'biliti/

n. 能力,才干

The ability to be clearly heard is extremely important for news-readers. 声音洪亮清晰对新闻播音员来说极为重要。

衍 able *adj.*

同 capability

反 impotence

damage
/'dæmidʒ/

v. 损害;毁坏

The factory was extensively damaged in the earthquake. 这家工厂在地震中遭到巨大破坏。

衍 damaging *adj.*

同 destroy

搭配 do/cause damage to 损坏(房屋等);毁坏(名誉等)

identical
/ai'dentikəl/

adj. 同一的,相同的

The copy was identical with the original.
复制本和原件完全一样。

同 exact

反 distinct, dissimilar

搭配 be identical with 相同的,一模一样的

race
/reis/

n. & v. 赛跑;和……竞赛

They are in a race against time.
他们在和时间赛跑。

搭配 race about/around 在……来回奔走

abnormal
/æb'nɔːməl/

adj. 反常的,变态的

Sometimes this kid has abnormal behaviors.
有时候这个孩子会有一些反常的行为。

同 eccentric, queer

反 normal

基础词汇

拓展词汇

campaign
/kæm'pein/

n. (军)战役,(政治或商业性)活动

Police have launched a campaign to crack down on drug dealers. 警方展开了一次严惩贩毒分子的行动。

同 strategy, battle

bachelor
/'bætʃələ/

n. 单身汉;文理学士

He remained a bachelor for seven years after his first wife's death. 他在第一个妻子死后当了7年单身汉。

cancel
/'kænsl/

vt. 取消,删去

His eccentric behavior canceled the good impression he had made previously. 他的古怪行为抵消了以前他给人留下的良好印象。

衍 cancellation *n.*

同 call off

jam
/dʒæm/

v. 堵塞

His foot was jammed between two rocks.
他的脚给卡在两块岩石中间了。

短语 get into a jam 陷入困境

keep up with

跟上(人,潮流,形势等)

My salary doesn't keep up with inflation.
我的工资跟不上通货膨胀。

obedient
/ə'biːdiənt/

adj. 服从的;孝顺的

A servant must be obedient to his master.
仆人须服从他的主人。

衍 obedience *n.*

同 compliant

反 rebellious, disobedient

paradox
/'pærədɔks/

n. 似非而是的论点；自相矛盾的话

The answer to the question is full of paradox.

他的回答矛盾百出。

衍 paradoxical *adj.*

同 contradiction

tag
/tæg/

n. 标签

Each coat in the store has a tag with the price on it.

店里的每一件上衣都有标签标出价格。

call off

取消；停止进行

Why was the meeting called off?

会议为什么取消了？

earnest
/'ə:nist/

adj. 认真的；热心的

Mary is an earnest student.

玛丽是个认真的学生。

衍 earnestly *adv.*

同 sincere, serious

反 careless

sacrifice
/'sækrifais/

v. 牺牲，献身

He sacrificed his life to save the child from the fire.

他为了从火中救出孩子而牺牲了自己的生命。

同 give up

parade
/pə'reid/

v. 游行；阅兵

The colonel paraded his soldiers.

上校集合士兵接受检阅。

拓展词汇

提高词汇

safeguard
/ˈseifˌɡɑːd/

n. & vt. 维护；捍卫

Keeping clean is a safeguard against disease.
保持清洁能预防疾病。

同 protect, defend

naive
/nɑiˈiːv/

adj. 天真的

Don't try to act naive with me.
别对我假装天真。

衍 naivety *n.*

同 innocent

反 sophisticated

sanction
/ˈsæŋkʃən/

n. 批准；认可

Official sanction has not yet been given.
尚未获得正式批准。

同 authorization, approval

反 ban, prohibition

waterproof
/ˈwɔːtəpruːf/

adj. 防水的，不透水的

This material is waterproof.
这种材料是防水的。

yield
/jiːld/

v. 生长；生产；屈服

This orchard yields apples and pears.
这座果园出产苹果和梨。

同 generate

反 resist

搭配 yield to 屈服，投降

fabulous
/ˈfæbjuləs/

adj. 难以置信的；极好的

We had a fabulous time at the garden party.

我们在游园会上玩得很痛快。

同 wonderful, excellent

反 ordinary

pace
/peis/

n. 步调；步态

He took three paces forward.

他向前跨了三步。

同 speed, step

短语 keep pace with 与……并驾齐驱

tackle
/ˈtækl/

v. 处理，解决

There is more than one way to tackle the problem.

处理这个问题的办法不止一种。

同 deal with

radiate
/ˈreidieit/

v. 放射；流露

There is tenderness that radiates from her.

在她身上可以感受到温柔。

衍 radiation *n.*

同 shine, illuminate

dart
/dɑːt/

v. 飞奔；投掷（飞镖）

Adam darted back into bed as his father's step was heard on the stairs. 比尔听见他爸爸上楼的脚步声，马上就跳回床上。

同 shoot, run

飞跃词汇

fabricate
/ˈfæbrikeit/

vt. 制作；虚构

The best craftsman fabricated this clock.
这只钟是手艺最好的工匠制作的。

衍 fabrication *n.*

同 produce

---

magnitude
/ˈmæɡnitjuːd/

n. 巨大；重要性

A decision of this magnitude had to have national support. 如此重大的决定必须得到全国的支持。

同 vastness

反 insignificance

unanimous
/juːˈnæniməs/

adj. 意见一致的，无异议的

He was elected by a unanimous vote.
他以全票当选。

衍 unanimity *n.*

同 universal

反 split, divided

UNIT 2

abolish
/ə'bɔliʃ/

vt. 废止，废除（法律、制度、习俗等）

The American Civil War abolished slavery.
美国内战废除了奴隶制。

衍 abolition *n.*
同 cancel
反 establish

debate
/di'beit/

v. & n. 争论，辩论

Parliament will debate the question tomorrow.
议会明天将辩论这个问题。

同 argue
搭配 debate upon/on 讨论
辨析 debate 讨论
argument 辩论；论证
controversy 有争议，不能达成共识

galaxy
/'gæləksi/

n. 星系；银河

I saw a galaxy of light on a hillside.
我看见山腰上有一片闪光。

maintain
/mein'tein/

vt. 维持；主张

The students find it difficult to maintain themselves on the grants they receive. 学生们感到光靠领到的助学金难以维持生活。

同 assert
反 stop, quit

narrow
/'nærəu/

adj. 狭窄的；眼光短浅的

The decision was taken for narrow economic reasons, without considering its social effects. 这一决定是从狭隘的经济方面的原因作出的，并没有考虑其社会效应。

反 broad, wide

object
/'ɔbdʒikt/

n. 物体；目的；宾语

There were various objects on the table.
桌子上有各式各样的物件。

短语 attain one's object 达到目的

particular
/pə'tikjulə/

adj. 特别的；独特的

There was nothing of particular importance in the E-mail. 这封电子邮件里没有什么特别重要的内容。

同 special, unusual

短语 in particular 特别，尤其

random
/'rændəm/

adj. 任意的；随便的

The opinion poll was based on a random sample of adults. 这次民意调查是在成人当中随机抽样进行的。

短语 at random 任意的

under
/'ʌndə/

prep. 在……之下

The bottle fell under the table.
瓶掉到桌子底下了。

candidate
/'kændidət/

n. 候选人

There were three candidates for the vacancy.
这一空缺有三名候选人。

同 nominee, contender

基础词汇

face
/feis/

n. 脸;面容;表情

He has become a familiar face in Washington D.C.
他在华盛顿已成为大家都熟悉的人物。

短语 face the music 承担自己行为的后果

take
/teik/

v. 拿,拿走;取

Go and take a larger spoon.
去拿一个大一点的匙来。

短语 take after 仿效

above all

最重要;首先

I should like to rent a house—modern, comfortable and above all, in a quiet location. 我想租一幢房子,要求设备现代化,舒适,尤其是地段要清静。

capacity
/kə'pæsiti/

n. 容量;能力

The stadium has a seating capacity of 18,000.
这个体育场能容纳18000名观众。

同 competence

raise
/reiz/

v. 提高;抬高

The blocks raise the table three inches.
垫块把桌子抬高了三英寸。

同 increase, advance

participation
/pɑːˌtisi'peiʃən/

n. 参与

The success of the festival depended upon the participation of the whole community. 节日活动的成功有赖于全社区的积极参与。

衍 participate v.

同 take part in

10

拓展词汇

back
/bæk/

v. 后退；支持
The car backed through the gate.
汽车倒车开出大门。
反 front

ecology
/i(:)'kɔlədʒi/

n. 生态学
The ecology movement is going on in the city.
城里正在进行生态保护运动。

halt
/hɔːlt/

n. 停止；暂停
The car came to a sudden halt.
汽车突然停了下来。
同 stop, termination
短语 come to a halt 停止

idleness
/'aidlnis/

n. 闲散，懒惰，赋闲无事
The team will be of idleness tomorrow.
这个队明天轮空无赛事。
衍 idle *adj.*
搭配 idle away 虚度

kill off

消灭
The factory dumped poisonous wastes into the river and killed off the fish. 工厂把有毒的废弃物倒入河中，把鱼都杀死了。

lace
/leis/

v. 用带子系
These shoes are laced up the side.
这些鞋子是在旁边穿鞋带的。

quarter
/'kwɔːtə/

n. 四分之一
The programme lasted an hour and a quarter.
节目持续了一小时十五分钟。

scan
/skæn/

v. 浏览;扫描

He scanned the headlines of today's newspaper.
他浏览了今天报纸的大标题。

同 browse

take aback

吃惊

I was taken aback by his rudeness.
他那样粗鲁无理让我大吃一惊。

dazzle
/'dæzl/

v. (使)眼花;耀眼

I was dazzled by the car's headlights.
汽车前灯灯光使我目眩。

parallel
/'pærəlel/

adj. 平行的;并联的

The road runs parallel with the railway.
该公路与铁路平行。

搭配　run parallel with 和……平行

capability
/ˌkeipə'biliti/

n. (实际)能力;容量

The workers in this company are promoted according to their capabilities. 这家公司的工人是根据他们的能力得到提升的。

衍 capable *adj.*

同 ability

jeopardize
/'dʒepədaiz/

v. 危害

Would such legislation jeopardize the chances for a treaty? 制订这样的法律会危及签约的可能性吗?

衍 jeopardy *n.*

同 endanger, threaten

12

waver
/'weivə/

vi. 摆动；犹豫

The palm trees wavered in the wind.
棕榈树在风中摇曳。

衍 wavering *adj.*

同 shake, flutter

abortion
/ə'bɔːʃən/

n. 流产；夭折

His plan proved an abortion.
他的计划中途夭折。

衍 abortive *adj.*

同 miscarriage

eccentric
/ik'sentrik/

adj. 行为古怪的

His eccentric behavior lost him his job.
他怪癖的行为使他丢了工作。

衍 eccentricity *n.*

同 weird

反 normal

identity
/ai'dentiti/

n. 身份

There is no clue to the identity of the thief.
没有确定的有关窃贼身份的线索。

rage
/reidʒ/

n. 狂暴；大怒

The wind is a rage. 狂风肆虐。

同 anger, wrath

反 delight

短语 fly into a rage 勃然大怒

sane
/seɪn/

adj. 健全的
No sane man would do that.
神志正常的人谁也不会那么做。
衍 saneness *n.*
同 rational, clear-thinking
反 crazy

savage
/'sævidʒ/

adj. 野蛮的，未开化的；凶猛的
The elephant can be quite savage.
象会大发野性。
同 brutal, fierce
反 tame, civilized

captive
/'kæptiv/

n. 俘虏
These captives will be taken to the rear areas.
这些俘虏将被押到后方。
短语 take captive 活捉

facet
/'fæsit/

n. (多面体的)面；方面
He has traveled extensively around the world, recording every facet of life. 他游历了世界上很多地方，记录了生活的方方面面。
同 aspect, angle

vacuum
/'vækjuəm/

n. 真空
Her husband's death left a vacuum in her life.
丈夫的去世使她的生活变得空虚。
同 emptiness, blankness

partial
/'pɑːʃl/

adj. 偏爱的；局部的，不完全的
A parent should not be partial to any one of his children.
父母不应偏袒自己孩子中的任何一个。
衍 partiality *n.*
同 incomplete, limited
反 complete
搭配 be partial to 对……偏爱

UNIT 3

carry away

使激动而失去自制力
The film was so wonderful that she was completely carried away. 影片十分精彩,她完全被吸引住了。

---

decay
/di'kei/

v. (使)腐朽;衰退,衰落
His teeth began to decay.
他的牙齿已开始蛀蚀。
同 decline, deteriorate
反 thrive

---

economy
/i'kɔnəmi/

n. 经济;节约
We are having an economy drive at school.
我们学校正开展节约运动。
衍 economical *adj.*
同 thriftiness
反 lavishness

---

gangster
/'gæŋstə/

n. (美俗)歹徒,土匪,强盗
Gangster films are popular.
描写盗匪的影片很受欢迎。
同 mobster, hoodlum

---

lack
/læk/

v.& n. 缺乏
She lacks experience. 她缺乏经验。
同 want, deficiency
反 abundance
搭配 for lack of 因缺乏……

15

majestic
/mə'dʒestik/

adj. 宏伟的;庄严的

In the distance rose the majestic Alps.
远处崛起巍峨的阿尔卑斯山。

同 grand

反 humble

obligation
/ˌɔbli'geiʃən/

n. 义务;职责

The manufacturer has not fulfilled the terms of his obligation. 这位制造商未能履行合同的条款。

同 responsibility

partner
/'pɑ:tnə/

n. 合伙人;伴侣

She was made a partner in the firm.
她当上了该商行的股东。

同 collaborator

range
/reindʒ/

n. 范围 *v.* 处在……范围内

For more than 20 years, we've been supporting educational programs that range from kindergartens to colleges. 20多年来,我们一直在支持从幼儿园到大学的各种教育项目。

同 scope

scar
/skɑ:/

v. & n. 使留下伤痕;创伤

The cut on his finger will eventually scar over.
他手指上的伤口最终将会愈合。

同 wound

absent
/'æbsənt/

adj. 不在的,缺席的

I will be absent from work tomorrow.
明天我不上班。

衍 absence *n.*

反 present

16

career
/kə'riə/

n. 事业，生涯

His career opportunities suddenly looked brighter.
他突然又有希望飞黄腾达了。

同 profession

carve
/kɑːv/

v. 雕刻；切开

John carved his initials on the tree.
约翰把他姓名的首字母刻在树上了。

同 cut

ignorant
/'ignərənt/

adj. 无知的

She was ignorant about these people round her husband.
她对丈夫周围这些人全然不了解。

衍 ignorance *n.*

同 unfamiliar, uneducated

反 learned

搭配 be ignorant of 不知道的

rare
/reə/

adj. 稀罕的；珍贵的

Snow is rare in this region.
这地区难得下雪。

同 unusual, scarce

反 common, usual

rank
/ræŋk/

v. 排列；归类于

I rank her among the country's best writers.
我认为她可属全国最优秀作家之列。

同 classify

scatter
/'skætə/

v. 分散；驱散

The wind soon scattered the clouds. 风起云散。

同 distribute

反 gather

abrupt
/ə'brʌpt/

adj. 突然的；陡峭的

He made an abrupt turn to avoid hitting another car.
他猛地一个急转弯，以免撞上另一辆汽车。

衍 abruptness *n.*

同 sudden, unexpected

反 anticipated

facilitate
/fə'siliteit/

vt. (不以人作主语的)使容易，使便利

Such a port would facilitate the passage of oil from the middle East to Japan. 这样一个港口将会使中东至日本的石油运输变得便捷。

同 simplify, ease

反 hinder, hamper

jerk
/dʒəːk/

n. 急推；猛拉

He shut the drawer with a jerk.
他猛地关上抽屉。

同 pull, yank

短语 in a jerk 立刻，马上

knot
/nɔt/

v. 使紧张；使缠结

My stomach knotted at the news.
听到这消息我的心揪紧了。

短语 tie the knot 结婚（主持婚礼）

navigation
/ˌnævi'geiʃən/

n. 航海；导航

There has been an increase in navigation through the Panama Canal. 经过巴拿马运河的船只有所增加。

衍 navigate *v.*

同 steering

get by

勉强对付；妥善处理

How does she get by on such a small salary?
她靠这么一点儿薪水怎么过活？

underestimate
/ˌʌndəˈestimeit/

vt. 低估；看轻

Don't underestimate your opponent.
不要轻视你的对手。

同 underrate, belittle

反 exaggerate, overestimate

in case of

防备；假使

The wall was built along the river in case of floods.
沿河筑了防护墙以防洪水。

absorb
/əbˈsɔːb/

vt. 吸收；吸引

His active mind was a sponge, absorbing impressions and information. 他那活跃的头脑像块海绵，能吸入种种印象和信息。

衍 absorption *n.*

同 assimilate

反 spit out

搭配 be absorbed in 专注于

take effect

见效；生效

His appointment takes effect from March 1.
他的任命自3月1日起生效。

pass through

经历

He eventually became successful after passing through hardships. 遭受过苦难后，他终于成功了。

quit
/kwit/

v. 辞职;放弃

Quit grumbling! 别抱怨了!

同 give up

反 start, begin

wear off

逐渐减弱;消失;耗损

The novelty will wear off.
新鲜感会慢慢消失。

deceive
/di'si:v/

v. 欺骗,行骗

We will not deceive you in this matter.
在这件事上我们绝不骗你。

衍 deceit *n.*

同 defraud

搭配 deceive sb. into doing 骗某人做某事

facility
/fə'siliti/

n. 灵巧,熟练;便利

Parctice gives a wonderful facility.
娴熟的技巧来自于实践。

同 efficiency

partition
/pɑː'tiʃən/

vt. 分割;瓜分

India was partitioned in 1947.
印度于1947年分裂。

同 separate, divide

提高词汇

scarcity
/'skɛəsiti/

n. 缺乏, 不足

The scarcity of supplies was alleviated when new shipments arrived. 新来了几批货物使供应不足得到了缓解。

衍 scarce *adj.*

同 deficiency

反 abundance

搭配 a scarcity of 缺少, 不足

辨析 scarce 以前很多, 现在变得稀少
　　rare 稀罕的, 含有贵重的意思

take in

理解; 接受

I hope you are taking in what I am saying.
我希望你能听得进去我说的话。

scare
/skeə/

v. 惊吓, 惊恐

He scares easily. 他动不动就害怕。

同 frighten

反 reassure

搭配 scare away 把……吓跑

飞跃词汇

badge
/bædʒ/

n. 徽章; 象征

Chains are a badge of slavery. 镣铐是奴役的象征。

同 emblem, symbol

hamper
/'hæmpə/

v. 妨碍, 牵制

Why do you want to go and hamper yourself with such a man? 你为什么要去受这样一个家伙的牵累呢?

同 hinder, obstruct

反 facilitate, assist

21

飞跃词汇

ignite
/ig'nait/

v. 点火;点燃

The candle ignited the plastic and started a small fire.

蜡烛引燃了塑料,引起了一场小火灾。

衍 ignition *n.*

同 kindle

反 extinguish, smother

短语 ignition point 燃点

vague
/veig/

adj. 含糊的,不清楚的;茫然的

The final letter is very vague ; possibly an R or K .

最后一个字母很不清楚,可能是R或是K。

衍 vagueness *n.*

同 ambiguous

反 clear

UNIT 4

cash
/cæʃ/

n. 现金
I have no cash with me. Can I pay by cheque?
我身边没带钱,付支票行吗?
同 money

decent
/'diːsnt/

adj. 正派的;有分寸的
She did not have a decent dress for the ball.
她没有参加舞会的合适衣服。
衍 decency *n.*
同 proper
反 notorious

effective
/i'fektiv/

adj. 有效的;显著的
Light clothes are effective in keeping cool in warm weather. 热天穿浅色衣服能使人感到凉快。
同 productive
反 impotent

gap
/gæp/

n. 缺口;间隙;差距
The gap between the rich and the poor widens.
贫富之间的差距在扩大。
短语 bridge the gap between... 消除……的隔阂;
缩小……的差距

hand
/hænd/

n. 手;协助;帮手
The project requires many hands.
这项工程需要许多人手。
同 aide, assistant
短语 at hand 近在手边

ignore
/ig'nɔː/

vt. 不理睬,忽视
My driving was suspended for ignoring a red light.
我因为闯红灯而被罚暂停驾驶。
同 neglect
反 notice

make
/meik/

v. 制造
The toy is made of animal skins.
这些玩具是由兽皮制作的。
同 create
短语 make do 勉强应对

necessity
/ni'sesiti/

n. 必要性;必需品
There is no necessity for disappointment. 不必失望。
衍 necessary *adj.*
同 must
反 inessential

oblige
/ə'blaidʒ/

vt. 迫使;强制
The law obliges parents to send their children to school.
法律规定父母有义务送孩子上学。
同 compel

quiver
/'kwivə/

v. 震动;颤抖
The leaves quivered in the breeze.
树叶在微风中颤动。
同 shake, tremble

rate
/reit/

n. 比率；速度

At this rate, we shall soon be bankrupt.
这样下去的话，我们很快就要破产了。

同 speed
搭配 at the rate of 以……的速度
短语 at any rate 无论如何

---

weep
/wiːp/

v. 哭泣，落泪

He wept over his dead brother.
他哀悼自己的亡兄。

同 cry

---

absurd
/əbˈsəːd/

adj. 荒谬的，可笑的

Even sensible men do something absurd sometimes.
即使是理智的人，有时候也会做出荒谬的事情来。

衍 absurdity *n.*
同 ridiculous
反 rational, sensible
辨析 absurd 形容显然与常识和理性相反
　　foolish 愚蠢的，无知的
　　ridiculous 有轻蔑和嘲笑的意味

Week①Day④

---

factor
/ˈfæktə/

n. 因素，要素

Endurance is an important factor of success in sports.
耐力是运动中取得胜利的重要因素。

同 element

---

scenery
/ˈsiːnəri/

n. 风景，景色

The scenery is imposing. 景色壮丽。
辨析 scenery 一个地区的总的自然景色
　　sight 风景，名胜
　　landscape 风景，山水

基础词汇

scene
/siːn/

n. 现场；场面
The scene of this opera is laid in Switzerland.
这部歌剧的场景安排在瑞士。
同 location
搭配 on the scene 在场，到场

abstract
/'æbstrækt/

adj. 抽象的；深奥的
A flower is beautiful, but beauty itself is abstract.
花是美丽的，可美丽本身则是抽象的。
衍 abstraction *n.*
反 concrete

faculty
/'fæklti/

n. 才能，本领；全体教员
His faculty of hearing is acute.
他的听觉灵敏。
同 aptitude

lane
/lein/

n. (乡间)小路；巷子
It is a long lane that has no turning.
路必有弯。
同 path, road

patent
/'peitənt/

n. 专利权；专利品
Patents have been running out on these drugs.
这些药的专利权正在先后到期。
同 licence

undergo
/ˌʌndə'gəu/

vt. 经历；遭受
His opinions underwent a change.
他的看法起了变化。
同 experience, go through

valid
/'vælid/

adj. (律)有效的;有根据的;正当的

This was the real reason, and it was a valid reason.

这是真实的也是令人信服的理由。

同 legitimate

反 invalid

decline
/di'klain/

v. 下降;拒绝;衰败

She declined to address the delegates.

她谢绝给代表们讲话。

同 reject

反 accept

搭配 be on the decline 下降,减少

abundant
/ə'bʌndənt/

adj. 丰富的,充裕的

These plants are abundant in the tropics.

这些植物在热带很多。

衍 abundance *n.*

同 plentiful

反 scarce

搭配 abundant in 丰富的,富裕的

辨析 abundant 丰富的,充足的,主要修饰自然物质

plentiful 超过充分供应的,绰绰有余的

sufficient 充分的,足够的

scheme
/ski:m/

n. & v. 安排;计划;阴谋

He suggested several schemes to increase sales.

他提出了几种促销的方案。

同 proposal, strategy

pat
/pæt/

v. 轻拍

He patted his face dry with a towel.

他用毛巾把脸擦干。

同 tap

rather than
与其……不如；不是……而是
He is a writer rather than a teacher.
与其说他是教师，不如说他是作家。

talent
/'tælənt/
n. 天才；才干，才能
This sort of work calls for special talents.
做这种工作要求特殊的才干。
同 genius, gift

take up
拿起；开始从事
He took up a weekly and began to read.
他拿起一本周刊读了起来。

casualty
/'kæʒuəlti/
n. 伤亡
Many casualties occurred during the accident.
这起事故有许多人伤亡。
同 fatality

catch up on
弥补
He has to catch up on his studies in the holiday.
他必须在假期补习功课。

efficiency
/i'fiʃənsi/
n. 效率
Different skills are taught to the students in the schools to develop the efficiency of their reading. 学校教学生各种阅读技能，以提高他们的效率。
衍 efficient *adj.*
反 inefficiency
辨析 efficient 效率高的 competent 能胜任的

illusion
/i'luːʒn/

n. 幻觉;错觉;假象

It is time for them to cast aside their illusions.
现在该是他们丢掉幻想的时候了。

同 delusion

passionate
/'pæʃənit/

adj. 热情的;易动情的

She burst into passionate sobbing.
她突然激动地抽泣不止。

衍 passion *n.*

同 enthusiastic

pastime
/'pɑːstaim/

n. 消遣,娱乐

Golf is his favotire pastime.
高尔夫是他最喜爱的娱乐。

同 hobby

ratio
/'reiʃiəu/

n. 比率

The ratio of the pupils to teachers was 30 to 1.
学生和老师比例是30比1。

同 proportion

baffle
/'bæfl/

vt. 困惑;阻碍

The police admitted that they were baffled by the complexity of the case. 警察承认由于案情复杂,他们束手无策。

同 frustrate

junction
/'dʒʌŋkʃən/

n. 连接;汇合处

At the junction of two rivers, there are tall buildings.
在两条河流的交汇点有很多高楼。

同 connection

飞跃词汇

scavenge
/'skævindʒ/

v. 打扫;以……为食

They scavenged all kinds of food they could to keep alive. 他们能找到什么样的食物就捡什么来维持生命。

catastrophe
/kə'tæstrəfi/

n. 大灾难

Everyone hates the catastrophe of wars.
每个人都憎恨战争带来的灾难。

同 disaster, calamity

UNIT 5

balance
/'bæləns/

n. & v. 秤;天平;平衡

Most industries have inventories in balance with sales.
多数制造业拥有与销售额保持平衡的存货。

同 equilibrium

反 imbalance

短语 keep balance 保持平衡

decorate
/'dekəreit/

v. 装饰;为……做室内装修

My mum decorated the room with hollies for Christmas.
妈妈用冬青装饰房间迎圣诞。

衍 decoration n.

同 ornament

effort
/'efət/

n. 努力;精力

The school has spared no effort on facilities or staff.
学校在充实设备或人员方面不遗余力。

同 endeavor

短语 make an effort 努力

fade
/feid/

v. (声音等)减弱下去;褪色

The bloom in her cheeks had faded.
她脸颊上的红润光泽已经消退。

同 wane

反 brighten, increase

短语 fade away 逐渐消失

gaze
/geiz/

v. 盯,凝视

Mary is gazing at the ceiling.
玛丽目不转睛的看着天花板。

同 stare

搭配 gaze at 盯着看

justice
/ˈdʒʌstis/

n. 正义;公平

Liberty and justice for all!
给人人以自由和公正!

同 uprightness

反 unfairness, immorality

短语 bring to justice 把……送交法院审判

late
/leit/

adj. & adv. 迟的;晚(期)的;已故的

My brother often comes home late from football games, covered in cuts and bruises. 我弟弟常常踢球到很晚才回家,身上伤痕累累。

同 delayed

反 punctual

negative
/ˈnegətiv/

adj. 否定的;消极的

He has shown some negative kindness to me.
他对我的仁慈是有消极意味的。

同 opposing

反 positive

短语 in the negative 否定地

scholarship
/ˈskɔləʃip/

n. 奖学金;学识

I came to Harvard on a scholarship.
我是靠奖学金到哈佛大学来求学的。

同 fellowship

基础词汇

what
/wɔt/

pron. int. & n. 什么；怎么

I could not imagine what would happen next.
我不能想像接下来会发生什么事情。

acceptance
/ək'septəns/

n. 接受；赞同

I beg your acceptance of the gift.
我请求你收下这份礼物。

衍 accept *v.*

反 refusal

fail
/feil/

v. 失败；不及格

The patient's heart failed.
病人的心脏停止了跳动。

衍 failure *n.*

搭配　fail to do sth. 未做成某事

短语　without fail 务必

patience
/'peiʃəns/

n. 耐心，忍耐

She has endless patience with the children.
她对孩子非常有耐心。

衍 patient *adj.*

同 endurance

短语　Patience is a plaster for all sores. 忍耐可治万
　　　千痛。

reach
/riːtʃ/

v. 延伸到某处

The train reaches London at five.
这班列车五点到达伦敦。

raw
/rɔː/

adj. 未加工的

We can eat carrots cooked or raw.
胡萝卜可以煮了吃，也可以生吃。

基础词汇

拓展词汇

scope
/skəup/

n. (活动)范围，机会

In my opinion, you can widen your scope through active participation. 我认为你可以积极参与来扩大视野。

同 range, extent

abuse
/ə'bjuːz/

n. & v. 滥用；虐待；辱骂

He abused his privileges in activities outside his official capacity. 他在职务范围之外滥用特权。

同 ill-treatment

反 compliment

hand down

传递某物；把某物往下传

Please hand down that dictionary to me from the shelf. 请把书架上那本词典拿下来给我。

make out

理解；辨认出

I cannot make out his handwriting. 我不能辨认出他的字迹。

patrol
/pə'trəul/

v. & n. 出巡，巡逻；巡逻队

The patrol was changed at midnight. 巡逻者在午夜换班。

同 inspect, guard

rational
/'ræʃənl/

adj. & n. 理性的；合理的；有理数

Man is a rational being. 人是理性的动物。

同 reasonable, sensible

反 irrational

拓展词汇

talk into

说服某人做某事

He thought he could talk Mr. Robinson into buying some expensive equipment. 他觉得他能说服鲁滨逊先生买些昂贵的仪器。

vanish
/'væniʃ/

vi. 消失

The thief vanished in the crowd.
那小偷消失在人群中。

同 disappear

反 appear

accelerate
/ək'seləreit/

v. 加速;促进

The government accelerated a train by turning on more power. 政府增加动力使列车加快速度。

衍 acceleration *n.*

同 speed up

反 slow down

dedicate
/'dedikeit/

vt. 献(身);致力(于)

A monument was dedicated to the memory of the soldiers who had died there. 为纪念牺牲的士兵,一座纪念碑在那儿建了起来。

衍 dedication *n.*

同 devote

搭配 be dedicated to... 献身于……

eject
/i'dʒekt/

vt. 驱逐;喷射

The pilot ejected over Germany when his engine stopped. 驾驶员在发动机停止运转时,在德国上空弹射出来。

同 oust

tame
/teim/

adj. & vt. 驯养,驯服;柔顺的

He made quite a name for himself by taming hawks.
他因驯鹰而使自己扬名。

同 docile, domestic

反 wild

patriotic
/ˌpætri'ɔtik/

adj. 爱国的

He is very patriotic and doesn't tolerate any insult to his country. 他很爱国,不能容忍别人对自己祖国的任何侮辱。

衍 patriotism *n.*

同 loyal

underline
/ˌʌndə'lain/

v. 在下面划线;强调

In writing, we underline titles of books.
在书写中,我们在书名下划线。

同 emphasize

cease
/siːs/

v. 停止

The music ceased suddenly. 音乐戛然而止。

同 terminate

反 begin

短语 without cease 不停的,不断的

caution
/'kɔːʃən/

n. & vt. 小心,谨慎,警告;警告

You must exercise extreme caution when crossing this road. 穿过这条马路时,你得特别小心。

衍 cautious *adj.*

同 prudence

反 carelessness

短语 do sth. with caution 小心谨慎地做某事

imaginary
/i'mædʒinəri/

adj. **想象的, 虚构的**

The equator is an imaginary circle around the earth.
赤道即假想的环绕地球的大圆。

同 visionary

反 real

辨析 imaginative 想象力丰富的

pathetic
/pə'θetik/

adj. **可怜的, 悲惨的**

The final scene of the movie is very pathetic.
这部电影的最后一幕十分凄惨。

衍 pathetically *adv.*

同 sorrowful

scrap
/skræp/

n. **碎片; 废料**

A man comes round regularly collecting scrap.
有个男人定时来收破烂。

scrape
/skreip/

v. **刮除, 擦掉**

She is scraping the path clear of snow.
她正在把路上的积雪铲掉。

incidentally
/ˌinsi'dentəli/

adv. **附带地, 顺便提及**

Some people, and incidentally that includes Arther, just won't look after themselves properly. 有些人, 比如说阿瑟吧, 就是不能好好自理。

同 by the way

catch on

理解;流行
That new song will catch on quickly.
那首新歌很快就会流行起来。

illustrate
/'iləstreit/

vt. & vi. 举例说明;图解
These graphs illustrate the results of the experiment.
这些图表说明实验的结果。
衍 illustration *n.*
同 explain

obscure
/əb'skjuə/

adj. 模糊的,晦涩的
Very few people could understand the lecture the professor delivered because its subject is very obscure.
教授演讲的主题含糊难懂,很少有人能够理解。
衍 obscurity *n.*
同 ambiguous
反 clear

celebrity
/si'lebriti/

n. 名声;名人
Jordon is a global celebrity. 乔丹是全球闻名的人。
同 fame

UNIT 6

bald
/bɔːld/

adj. 光秃的；单调的

He was starting to bald noticeably.
他明显地开始脱发。

同 bare
反 hairy

deem
/diːm/

v. 认为；相信

He did not deem lightly of the issue.
他对这个问题并没有掉以轻心。

同 consider

immediately
/i'miːdiətli/

adv. 立即，马上

She answered almost immediately.
她几乎当下就答复了。

同 instantly

imitate
/'imiteit/

v. 模仿，仿效

His handwriting is difficult to imitate.
他的笔迹很难模仿。

衍 imitation *n.*
同 copy, mimic

lately
/'leitli/

adv. 近来，最近

Have you seen him lately?
你最近见过他吗？

同 recently

Week❶Day❻

neglect
/ni'glekt/

vt. & n. 忽视，疏忽
They neglected his warning.
他们把他的警告当作耳旁风。

同 ignore

observe
/əb'zɜːv/

vt. 观察；遵守
She pretended not to observe it.
她装作没看见的样子。

衍 observation *n.*
同 notice

pattern
/'pætən/

n. 式样；模式
This student is a pattern of what a good student should be. 这个学生是好学生的一个样板。

同 form, sample

taste
/teist/

v. & n. 品尝；领略
Their trip to America gave them a taste for western consumer goods. 他们的美国之行使他们有机会品尝西方的消费品。

同 flavor

whereas
/(h)weər'æz/

conj. 然而；反之
She is diligent, whereas he is lazy.
她很勤快，而他却懒惰。

accommodate
/ə'kɔmədeit/

v. 向……提供；容纳；适应
When you get to a strange country, you'll have to accommodate yourself to a new way of living. 到外国时，你就得使自己适应新的生活方式。

衍 accommodation *n.*
同 adjust, accustom

faithfully
/'feiθfəli/

adv. 忠诚地

This dictionary has faithfully reflected changes in a living language. 这部辞典如实地记录了活的语言的变化。

衍 faithful *adj.*

同 devotedly, truthfully

pea
/piː/

n. 豌豆

New peas are delicious. 新鲜的豌豆很好吃。

ready
/'redi/

adj. 有准备的;现成的

Lunch will be ready in ten minutes.
午饭10分钟后开饭。

pause
/pɔːz/

n. & vi. 中止,暂停

The woman spoke almost without pausing for breath.
那女人说话像放连珠炮似的。

同 stop, halt

反 continue

reality
/ri(ː)'æliti/

n. 真实;事实

The plan will soon become a reality.
这计划不久就会变为现实。

access
/'ækses/

n. (进入某地的)方法;通路

The people living in these apartments have free access to that swimming pool. 住在这些公寓的人们可以免费使用那个游泳池。

同 approach

搭配 have access to 有接近(进入)的机会

cement
/si'ment/

v. 巩固;粘牢

This agreement has cemented our friendship.
这项协定巩固了我们的友谊。

同 bind, glue

fairly
/'feəli/

adv. 相当地;适度地

The book is fairly difficult. 这本书相当的难。

handy
/'hændi/

adj. 手边的,就近的

Keep a dictionary handy. 手边备一本词典。

同 accessible

短语 come in handy 派得上用处

justify
/'dʒʌstifai/

v. 证明……是正当的

A high turnover may well have been justified in view of volatile markets. 考虑到市场的多变,大成交量也许是很合理的。

同 vindicate

reaction
/ri(ː)'ækʃən/

n. 反应

I looked at Chris, trying to know his reaction.
我看着克里斯,试图估量他会作出什么反应。

衍 react *v.*

同 response

certificate
/sə'tifikət/

n. 证书;证明书

She could surely take the mood as a certificate that all was well. 她肯定会把这种情绪看作一种顺利的证明。

拓展词汇

chair
/tʃeə/

n. & vt. 椅子；主席；主持
Over 450 people attended the Sunday evening banquet and after-dinner program chaired by Hellen. 450多人参加了由海伦主持的星期日晚宴和饭后余兴节目。

peak
/piːk/

n. 山顶，顶点
The mountain peak was covered with snow all the year. 山峰终年积雪。

同 climax, top

seal
/siːl/

n. & vt. 封条；密封
We sealed up our windows in winter with slips of paper. 我们在冬天用纸条把窗缝密封起来。

短语 seal of office 公章

secondary
/ˈsekəndəri/

adj. 次要的
That problem is secondary to the one now facing us. 那个问题与我们目前所面临的问题相比是次要的。

同 subordinate, inferior
反 primary, main

solid
/ˈsɔlid/

adj. 固体的
Ice is water in a solid form. 冰是水的固体形态。

同 hard, compact
反 fluid

提高词汇

make up

弥补；虚构；化妆
The story is partly true and partly made up.
这个故事的内容一部分是真实的，一部分是杜撰的。

Week❶Day❻

43

scratch
/skrætʃ/

n. & v. 刮擦声;乱涂

Hens scatch in the ground. 母鸡在地上扒土。

搭配　scratch the surface 对待问题不深入,不彻底

短语　Scratch my back and I will scratch yours. 你帮助我,我也帮助你。

undertake
/ˌʌndə'teik/

vt. 承担,担任

We could undertake the work for the time being.
我们可以暂时承担此项工作。

同　take on, engage in

certify
/'sə:tifai/

v. 证明;保证

I can certify that the news is true and accurate.
我保证这条新闻准确无误。

同　verify

elaborate
/i'læbərət/

v. 详细阐述

He declined to elaborate. 他不愿详谈。

衍　elaboration *n.*

同　explain

deduction
/di'dʌkʃən/

n. 减除;推论

No deduction in pay is made for the absence due to illness. 因病不能上班的,不扣其工资。

衍　deduct *v.*

同　inference

tangle
/'tæŋgl/

n. 混乱状态

The wool got in a fearful tangle.
毛线乱成了一团。

同　mess

提高词汇

飞跃词汇

variable
/'veəriəbl/

adj. 易变地

The speed of the windscreen wipers is variable.
汽车挡风玻璃上刮水器的速度是可变的。

同 changeable

反 fixed

elapse
/i'læps/

v. (时间)消逝；流逝

Three years elapsed before he returned.
过了三年他才回来。

同 go by

gear
/giə/

v. 调整,(使)适合

Many football teams are not geared up to attack.
许多足球队不适应打攻势足球。

acclaim
/ə'kleim/

v. & n. 喝彩,欢呼

They acclaimed him as president.
他们欢呼拥戴他为总统。

同 applaud

反 disapprove

scrutiny
/'skruːtini/

n. 详细审查

His work looks all right, but it will not bear scrutiny.
他的工作看上去不错，但是经不起细察。

同 inspection, examination

UNIT 7

bankruptcy
/'bæŋkrʌptsi/

n. 破产

The company went into bankruptcy.
那家公司宣告破产了。

衍 bankrupt *adj.*

短语 go into bankruptcy 破产

defect
/'diːfekt/

n. 过失；缺点

It was a defect in her charcter.
那是她性格上的缺点。

同 flaw

搭配 in defect of 假如没有……时

electrician
/ilek'triʃ(ə)n/

n. 电工；电学家

The electrician repairs the electric fan skillfully.
电工很熟练地修着电风扇。

generalize
/'dʒenərəlaiz/

vt. 归纳，概括

You can not generalize about the effects of the drug from one or two cases. 不能根据一两个病例就得出该药是否有效的结论。

衍 generalization *n.*

immerse
/i'məːs/

vt. 沉浸；使陷入

He immersed himself totally in his work.
他埋头于工作。

同 submerge, sink

搭配 be immersed in 使专心于

46

基础词汇

realize
/ˈriəlaiz/

vt. 认识到，了解
She realized that he had been lying.
她明白了他一直在说谎。
衍 realization *n.*
同 perceive

sensitive
/ˈsensitiv/

adj. 敏感的；灵敏的
The film is not suitable for people of a sensitive disposition. 天性敏感的人不宜观看这部电影。
同 responsive
反 numb

tell
/tel/

v. 告诉
He told the news to everyone in the village.
他把那消息告诉了全村的人。

variety
/vəˈraiəti/

n. 变化，多样
The weatherman broadcasts the variety in temperature twice a day. 气象员一天播两次温度的变化。
同 diversity
反 sameness

whichever
/witʃˈevə/

pron. 无论那一个，任何一个
He may choose whichever he wishes.
他可以任选一个。

accordingly
/əˈkɔːdiŋli/

adv. 因此，从而
I have told you the rules, so you must act accordingly.
我已把规则告诉你了，所以你一定得照着做。
同 correspondingly

Week①Day⑦

character
/'kærɪktə/

n. (事物的)特性,性质;(人的)品质

He is a man of lofty character.
他是个品德高尚的人。

同 personality

immense
/ɪ'mens/

adj. 极广大的,无边的

The play was staged with immense success.
该剧上演获得巨大成功。

同 huge, gigantic

反 tiny

reason
/'riːzn/

n. 理由;理智

What was the reason for his being late?
他迟到的原因是什么?

同 cause

sense
/sens/

n. & vt. 官能;感觉

Sight, hearing, touch, taste, and smell are the five senses.
视觉、听觉、触觉、味觉、嗅觉合称五种官能。

短语 in a sense 从某种意义上说

soon
/suːn/

adv. 立刻,不久

I'd confidently predicted that they'd win, but I spoke too soon, they were beaten in the final race. 我曾经信心十足地预言他们会赢,但我讲得太早了,他们在决赛的时候被打败了。

accomplish
/ə'kɒmplɪʃ/

vt. 完成;实现

At that rate we'll accomplish only half the distance.
照这样的速度我们只能完成一半的路程。

衍 accomplishment *n.*

同 achieve

challenge
/'tʃælindʒ/

n. & vt. 挑战

They soon recognized the nature of the Conservative's challenge. 他们很快就意识到保守党挑战的性质了。

衍 challenging *adj.*

同 provocation

短语 rise to the challenge 奋起应付挑战

fame
/feim/

n. & vt. 名声,名望

He was famed for his ruthlessness.
他以冷酷无情出名。

同 reputation

搭配 be famed for 以……出名

hang on

坚持;有赖于

Hang on at your present job until you can get another.
你在没找到另一个工作前,不要放弃目前的工作。

account for

解释,说明(原因)

We must account for every cent we have spent.
我们对花掉的每一分钱都要有个交待。

peculiar
/pi'kjuːliə/

adj. 奇特的;特殊的

He has always been a little peculiar.
他为人总是有点古怪。

同 distinctive, queer

反 common

unexpectedly
/ˌʌnik'spektidli/

adv. 出乎意料地,想不到地

He entered the room unexpectedly.
他出人意料地进到屋子里来了。

elect
/i'lekt/

v. 选举;选择

First-year students may elect French or German.
一年级学生可以选修法语或德语。

衍 election *n.*

同 select

fake
/feik/

v. 假装;伪造

He isn't really hurt, he is only faking.
他并未真正受伤,只不过是在装样子而已。

同 feign

辨析　fake 假的,冒充的　　false 虚假的,不真实的

pedestrian
/pi'destriən/

adj. 徒步的

We enjoy all pedestrain activities.
我们喜欢所有的步行活动。

penalty
/'penlti/

n. 处罚,罚款

Penalties for overdue books will be strictly enforced.
对图书逾期应予以重罚。

同 punishment

secure
/si'kjuə/

adj. & v. 安全的;可靠的;放心的

She felt secure only when both doors were locked.
只有两扇门都锁上了她才感到放心。

衍 security *n.*

同 safe

反 dangerous

negligible
/'neglidʒəbl/

adj. 可以忽略的

His knowledge of English is negligible.
他的英语知识少的可怜。

同 insignificant

提高词汇

obsess
/əb'ses/

v. 迷住；困扰

He is obsessed by money. 他财迷心切。

衍 obsession *n.*

同 preoccupy

反 ignore

搭配 be obsessed with 使着迷

accordance
/ə'kɔːdəns/

n. 一致，和谐

I am in accordance with him in this matter.
在这件事情上我同他意见是一致的。

搭配 in accordance with 依照，根据

default
/di'fɔːlt/

n. & v. 不履行责任，疏怠职责

They lost their best client by sheer default.
他们完全由于疏忽而失去了最好的顾客。

charge
/tʃɑːdʒ/

n. 费用

The price of the coal will vary according to how
expensive the freight charges are. 煤炭的价格将
随运费的变化而波动。

短语 in charge of 负责，主管

see to

保证；照料

The security of the goods must be seen to.
货物的安全必须得到保证。

peer
/piə/

n. 同等地位的人；同辈

As an orator, he had few peers.
作为一个演说家，很少有人与他匹敌。

同 fellow

Week①Day⑦

提高词汇

飞跃词汇

reassure
/riːəˈʃuə/

vt. 使……安心；使……恢复信心
His remarks reassured me. 听了他的话我释然了。
同 hearten, comfort
反 discourage
辨析 assure 使相信；保证
ensure 担保；使安全

manifestation
/ˌmænifesˈteiʃən/

n. 显示，表现
His smile was a manifestation of his joy.
他的微笑是他高兴的一种表现。
同 testimony

characteristic
/ˌkæriktəˈristik/

n. 特性，特征
Windy days are characteristics of March.
有风天气是三月的特征。
衍 characterize *v.*
同 character

tedious
/ˈtiːdiəs/

adj. 冗长乏味的
The arguments were tedious and complicated.
那些论点冗长而繁复。
同 boring, tiresome
反 interesting

predicament
/priˈdikəmənt/

n. 困境
He didn't know how to get out of his predicament.
他不知道怎样才能使自己摆脱困境。
同 plight

UNIT 8

bare
/beə/

adj. 赤裸的，无遮蔽的
He sleeps on bare ground.
他睡在不铺地毯的地板上。
同 naked
反 covered, dressed

defend
/di'fend/

vt. 防护；辩护
Emily defended Jack against the criticism.
埃米莉为杰克受到的批评进行辩解。
衍 defense *n.*
同 protect, support
反 offend, attack

harbor
/'hɑːbə/

n. & v. 海港；庇护
The child fled to the harbor of her father's arms.
那孩子逃到父亲的怀里躲着。
同 dock, pier

latest
/'leitist/

adj. 最近的
Have you heard the latest news?
你听说最新消息了吗?
短语 at latest 最迟

manner
/'mænə/

n. 礼貌；风格；方式
His manner showed his anger.
他的态度表明了他的愤怒。
同 style
短语 in like manner 同样地

基础词汇

rebel
/ri'bel/

n. & v. 造反者;反叛

The rebel prided him on his unorthodoxy.
这个叛逆者以其非正统观点自诩。

同 revolt

搭配 rebel against 反叛

sentence
/'sentəns/

vt. 宣判

Jone was sentenced to one year at hard labor.
约翰被判处1年的苦役。

while
/(h)wail/

n. & conj. 一会儿;当……的时候

I'll be back in a little while. 我马上就回来。

搭配 once in a while 偶尔

cheerful
/'tʃiəfəl/

adj. 愉快的,高兴的

It's wonderful to see you so cheerful.
看到你这么高兴太好了。

同 joyful

反 gloomy

chill
/tʃil/

n. & adj. 寒意;寒冷的

The bad news put a chill into us all.
这坏消息使我们大家感到扫兴。

同 cold

pension
/'penʃən/

n. & v. 养老金,退休金

They pensioned him off when they found a younger man for the job. 他们找到一名较为年轻的人做这项工作,就发养老金让他退休了。

基础词汇

temper
/'tempə/

n. & v. **性情；锻炼**

Hardships tempered his revolutionary will.
艰难困苦锻炼了他的革命意志。

同 harden

反 soften

短语 fly into a temper 发脾气

percentage
/pə'sentidʒ/

n. **百分比**

What is the percentage of nitrogen in the air?
空气中氮的百分比是多少?

generate
/'dʒenəˌreit/

vt. **产生；发生**

Delayed salary generated resentment.
迟发工资导致不满。

衍 generation *n.*

同 produce

separate
/'sepəreit/

adj. & v. **分开的，单独的；分开**

England is separated from France by the channel.
英法两国由英吉利海峡隔开。

衍 separation *n.*

同 break off

反 connect

tolerate
/'tɔləreit/

vt. **忍受，容忍**

I can not tolerate his rudeness.
我不能容忍他的粗鲁行为。

衍 toleration *n.*

同 endure

account
/ə'kaunt/

n. 计算，账目，说明

On no account should any money be given to a small child. 一点钱都决不能给小孩。

同 description

短语　　on account of 因为，由于

on no account 决不

chase
/tʃeis/

vt. 追赶

The police chased the escaping thief and caught him at last. 警察部门追捕逃跑的窃贼，终于把他逮住了。

同 go after

elegant
/'eligənt/

adj. 雅致的

She leads a life of elegant ease.
她过着优裕闲适的生活。

衍 elegance *n.*

同 graceful

immortal
/i'mɔːtl/

adj. 不朽的

The heroes of the people are immortal.
人民英雄永垂不朽。

衍 immortality *n.*

同 eternal

negotiate
/ni'gəuʃieit/

v. (与某人)商议，谈判

We negotiate with them about the date of the conference.
我们就会议的日期一事进行谈判。

衍 negotiation *n.*

同 bargain, discuss

obstacle
/'ɔbstəkl/

n. 障碍

International suspicion is the chief obstacle to world peace. 国与国之间的猜疑是世界和平的主要障碍。

同 obstruction

56

penetrate
/'penitreit/

v. 穿透;洞察

The knife penetrated his stomach.
刀子刺进他的胃部。

衍 penetration *n.*

temperament
/'tempərəmənt/

n. 气质,性情

His silent temperament prevents him from getting along with his classmates. 他沉默寡言的性格使自己与其他同学无法融洽相处。

同 disposition

vary
/'veəri/

v. 改变,变更

Old people don't like to vary their habits.
老年人不喜欢改变他们的积习。

同 differ

accurate
/'ækjurət/

adj. 正确的,精确的

You must be more accurate in your work.
你必须在工作中更加注意正确性。

衍 accuracy *n.*

同 precise

fare
/feə/

n. 费用;乘客

The taxi-driver had only three fares.
这个出租车司机今天晚上只载了三个乘客.

perceive
/pə'siːv/

v. 察觉;感知

Do you perceive what I mean? 你明白我的意思吗?

衍 perception *n.*

同 comprehend

57

unfold
/ʌn'fəuld/

v. 打开；显露
Buds unfold into flowers. 蓓蕾开花了。

---

cherish
/'tʃeriʃ/

vt. 珍爱，怀抱（希望等）
My parents cherish us and do everything for us.
我们的父母很珍爱我们，为我们做任何事情。
同 value
反 despise

---

elevate
/'eliveit/

vt. 举起，提拔
The word has been elevated from the status of slang
to colloquialism. 这个词已经从俚语上升到口语的
地位了。
同 uplift
反 degrade

impact
/'impækt/

n. & vt. 影响，效果；对……发生影响
Public opinion makes a significant impact on government policy. 舆论对政府政策产生重大影响。
同 influence
搭配 have an impact on 对……有影响

receipt
/ri'si:t/

n. 收条，收据
The receipts barely covered expenditures.
全部收入仅够偿付各项支出。

---

sentiment
/'sentimənt/

n. 多愁善感；感情
She has too much sentiment to be successful.
她感情太脆弱，做不成大事。
衍 sentimental *adj.*

58

提高词汇

飞跃词汇

spark
/spɑːk/

v. & n. 火花
Her eyes were sparking with anger.
她的双眼射出怒火。

---

vice
/vais/

n. 恶习；罪恶
Lying and cruelty are vices.
说谎和残暴都是道德败坏行为。
同 sin, evil

---

famine
/'fæmin/

n. 饥荒
The long drought was followed by months of famine.
久旱之后出现长达数月的饥荒。
同 starvation

accumulate
/ə'kjuːmjuleit/

v. 积聚，堆积
Dust soon accumulates in rooms that are not cleaned.
房间不打扫很快就积满灰尘。
衍 accumulation *n.*
同 amass
反 disperse

deficit
/'defisit/

n. 赤字；落后
The baseball team erased a 6-0 deficit.
这支棒球队刷去了一个6比0的落后记录。

---

recession
/ri'seʃən/

n. 撤回；不景气
The country is experiencing a period of recession and underemployment. 这个国家已经在经历一段时间的衰退和就业不足。
同 regression

59

UNIT 9

bargain
/'bɑ:gin/

n. & v. 讨价还价;特价品

Remember that customers don't bargain about prices in that city. 请记住在那个城市顾客都是不讨价还价的。

同 barter

短语 strike a bargain with 成交

fascination
/fæsi'neiʃ(ə)n/

n. 魅力;迷恋

The new songs possess a positive fascination over her audience. 这些新歌确实把观众给迷住了。

衍 fascinate *v.*

同 attraction

搭配 have a fascination for 对……有极大的吸引力

generous
/'dʒenərəs/

adj. 慷慨的,大方的

He was generous in his praise of their works.
他对他们的作品赞扬备至。

衍 generosity *n.*

同 bountiful

反 meager

harm
/hɑ:m/

vt. & n. 伤害,损害

There is no harm in trying. 不妨一试。

衍 harmful *adj.*

同 damage

反 benefit

短语 do sb. harm 损害

基础词汇

Week ② Day ②

latter
/ˈlætə/

adj. (两者中)后者的

Of the two choices, I prefer the latter.
两个选择中，我更喜欢后者。

network
/ˈnetwəːk/

n. 网络

We have well developed marketing networks.
我们已充分发展了销售网络。

occasion
/əˈkeiʒən/

n. 场合；时机

They met on three occasions. 他们曾三次相遇。

短语　on one occasion 一次

sequence
/ˈsiːkwəns/

n. 次序，顺序

Please keep the cards in seqence.
请把纸牌按顺序排好。

同　order

短语　in sequence 按顺序排列

vast
/vɑːst/

adj. 巨大的；辽阔的

The vast plains stretch for hundreds of miles.
平原绵延数百英里。

wipe
/waip/

v. 擦，揩

Wipe your shoes on the mat.
在擦鞋垫上擦擦你的鞋。

circumstance
/'sə:kəmstəns/

n. 环境;境况

The weather is a circumstance to be taken into considerration. 天气是要考虑是一个条件。

同 condition

短语 under no circumstances 无论如何不

---

fasten
/'fɑːsn/

v. 扎牢,扣住

Fasten your seat belts, please. 请系好安全带。

同 attach

反 loosen

---

perfect
/'pəːfikt/

adj. 完美的;使完美

The actor was perfect for the part.
由这位演员担任这一角色再好不过了。

衍 perfection *n.*

短语 Practice makes perfect. 熟能生巧。

---

performance
/pə'fɔːməns/

n. 履行;表演;表现

He failed miserably in the performance of his duty.
他干得很差,未能履行他的职责。

衍 perform *v.*

---

temporary
/'tempərəri/

adj. 暂时的,临时的

The wartime temporary houses will be replaced by permanent homes. 那些战时临时房屋将被永久性住宅所代替。

同 transient

反 permanent

---

view
/vjuː/

n. & v. 景色;观点

It was my first view of the ocean.
那是我第一次见到海洋。

短语 in view of 考虑到

拓展词汇

accuse
/ə'kjuːz/

vt. 控告
They accused her publicly of stealing their books.
他们公开指控她偷他们的书。

衍 accusation *n.*

同 blame

反 defend

搭配 accuse sb. of 控告某人

be absorbed in

(使)全神贯注
The children were so absorbed in their game that they did not notice the passage of time. 孩子们只顾玩,没注意到时间很快过去。

imperative
/im'perətiv/

n. & adj. 紧急的事;强制的;紧急的
Military orders are imperative and can not be disobeyed.
军令如山,不能违抗。

同 urgent

manual
/'mænjuəl/

n. & adj. 手册,指南;体力的
Please follow the manual instructions.
请按照手册说明做。

reciprocal
/ri'siprəkəl/

adj. 互惠的;互相起作用的
Kindness is generally reciprocal.
盛情通常是有来往的。

同 interdependent

反 independent

universally
/juːni'vəːsəli/

adv. 普遍地,全体地
This explanation is not yet universally accepted.
这种解释尚未被所有人接受。

definite
/'definit/

adj. 明确的；一定的

It's definite that he will come. 他肯定要来的。

同 precise

反 uncertain

eligible
/'elidʒəbl/

adj. 符合条件的，合格的

He is eligible for promotion. 他符合提拔的条件。

同 qualified

反 unsuitable

搭配 be eligible for 合格

cite
/sait/

vt. 引用，引证

He ended his speech by citing his indebtedness to those who helped him. 他以对帮助过他的人表示感激来结束他的讲话。

set about

开始，着手

After breakfast, she set about her household duties. 早餐后她开始做家务。

arise from

由……引起

His fear arises from ignorance.
他的恐惧是由于无知引起的。

arrive at

得出（结论），做出（决定）

The manager and the union leader have not arrived at a settlement. 经理与工会领导人尚未达成解决办法的共识。

提高词汇

perception
/pə'sepʃən/

n. 理解，感知，感觉

He had a clear perception of what was wrong with the computer, and soon fixed it. 他清楚计算机的毛病出在哪里，很快就把它修好了。

衍 perceive *v.*

同 comprehension

tempo
/'tempəu/

n. (音乐) 节拍；发展速度

His pace slowed to the tempo of his thoughts.
他边走边想，步子随着思绪放慢了。

同 speed

circulation
/ˌsəːkju'leiʃən/

n. 循环，流通

This newspaper has a daily circulation of 500,000.
这份报纸日发行量50万份。

衍 circulate *v.*

短语 in circulation 流通中

acquaint
/ə'kweint/

vt. 使熟知

She is acquainted with the elements of calculus inside out. 她对微积分的基础原理了解得很透彻。

衍 acquaintance *n.*

同 familiarize

短语 acquaint oneself with 了解

allow for

把……考虑在内

When he made the plan, he failed to allow for the unexpected. 他做计划时没有把意外情况考虑进去。

recipe
/'resipi/

n. 食谱

This book offers a collection of fish recipes.
这本书收集了很多鱼的烹制方法。

65

提高词汇

飞跃词汇

session
/'seʃən/

n. 会议

This year's session of congress was unusually long.
今年国会的会期特别长。

setback
/'setbæk/

n. 挫折

The patient had a setback in his recovery.
病人在康复的过程中又发生了反复。

同 frustration

反 progress

chronic
/'krɔnik/

adj. 慢性的；延续很长时间的

He is a chronic smoker. 他是个烟瘾很大的人。

同 long-term

反 short-term

defy
/di'fai/

vt. 不服从，公然反抗

He was going ahead defying all difficulties.
他不顾一切困难坚持下去。

同 oppose

反 obey

acknowledgement
/ək'nɔlidʒmənt/

n. 致谢；回信

We have had no acknowledgement of our letter yet.
我们还没接到去信的回执。

衍 acknowledge *v.*

同 recognition

reckless
/'reklis/

adj. 不计后果的

He's quite reckless of the consequences.
他完全不顾及后果。

同 regardless of

反 careful, cautious

短语 reckless of 不介意的

66

UNIT 10

acquire
/ə'kwaiə/

vt. **获得；学到**

His brow has acquired its first wrinkle.
他的额头已出现第一条皱纹。

同 gain

反 lose

---

barren
/'bærən/

adj. **不生育的；贫瘠的**

She is barren of creative spirit.
她缺乏创造精神。

同 sterile

反 fertile

---

delay
/di'lei/

v. & n. **耽搁，延迟**

We were delayed in a traffic jam.
我们因交通拥挤而迟到了。

同 put off

---

classify
/'klæsifai/

vt. **分类，分等**

English intonation patterns can be classified into two
types. 英语语调可分为两类。

同 categorize

---

else
/els/

adj. & adv. **别的，其他**

Who else did you see? 你还看见了谁?

搭配 or else 否则

基础词汇

genuine
/'dʒenjuin/

adj. 名副其实的；纯种的

This is a dog of the genuine Newfoundland breed.
这只狗是纽芬兰纯种狗。

同 authentic

harmony
/'hɑ:məni/

n. 协调；融洽

They live together in perfect harmony.
他们住在一起非常和睦。

衍 harmonious *adj.*

搭配 in harmony with 与……协调一致

launch
/lɔ:ntʃ/

v. 发射；发动，发起

He suddenly launched out at me for no reason at all.
他突然无端攻击我。

permission
/pə(:)'miʃən/

n. 许可，允许

By permission of the author, I cited a passage from his book. 经作者同意，我引用了书中的一段话。

衍 permit *vt.*

同 consent

反 ban

recognize
/'rekəgnaiz/

v. 认可；识别

I recognized him the minute I saw him.
我一见他就认出来了。

衍 recognition *n.*

同 acknowledge

delegate
/'deligeit/

n. & vt. 代表；委派……为代表

He delegated his scretary to show me the city.
他委派秘书陪我参观这个城市。

tender
/'tendə/

adj. 嫩的；温柔的

I patted the dog with tender hands.
我用手轻轻拍狗。

unless
/ən'les, ʌn'les/

conj. 如果不，除非

Unless the government agrees to give extra money, the theatre will have to close. 如果政府不同意提供更多的资金，该剧院将不得不关闭。

action
/'ækʃən/

n. & vt. 动作；（戏剧或书中）的情节

The measure is awaiting Senate action.
这项措施正等待参议院作出决定。

短语　take action 采取行动

Actions speak louder than words.
行动比言语更响亮。

recommend
/rekə'mend/

vt. 推荐；介绍

I can't get hold of any of the college textbooks he recommended. 他推荐的大学教材，我一本都弄不到。

衍 recommendation *n.*

同 advise

stubborn
/'stʌbən/

adj. 顽固的，固执的

You will have to push hard, for that door is a bit stubborn. 你得用力推才行，那门不太好开。

同 obstinate

反 compromising

compensate
/'kɔmpənseit/

v. 偿还，补偿

The firm compensated the injured worker for the time lost. 公司向受伤工人赔偿时间的损失。

衍 compensation *n.*

同 make up for

acute
/ə'kjuːt/

adj. 敏锐的

A human's eyesight is not as acute as that of an eagle.
人的视力不如鹰的视力敏锐。

同 sharp

反 dull

---

civilization
/ˌsivəlai'zeiʃən/

n. 文明；文化

The book explores the relationship between religion and civilization. 这部书探讨了宗教和文明之间的关系。

衍 civilized *adj.*

---

clear up

整理；放晴

It cleared up quickly after the rain.
雨后天气迅速放晴。

---

fatal
/'feitl/

adj. 致命的；重大的

Clear morning air is fatal for my health.
早晨清新的空气对我的健康无可或缺。

同 deadly

---

implication
/ˌimpli'keiʃən/

n. 含意，暗示

I resent your implication that my work is unsatisfactory.
你暗指我的工作不令人满意,这使我很烦恼。

同 inference

---

margin
/'mɑːdʒin/

n. 页边的空白；(湖、池等的)边缘

Mary sits on the margin of a swimming pool.
玛丽坐在游泳池的边上。

同 verge

反 center

短语 at the margin of 在……边缘

occasionally
/ə'keiʒənəli/

adv. 有时候,偶尔

He only smokes a cigar occasionally.
他难得抽支雪茄烟。

同 sometimes

severe
/si'viə/

adj. 严厉的;剧烈的

Her rejection came as a severe blow to his pride.
她的拒绝是对他自信心的沉重打击。

同 harsh

反 mild

tempt
/tempt/

vt. 诱惑;考验

His success tempted others to try the same way.
他的成功吸引了很多人走相同的路。

同 lure

反 repulse

辨析　tempt 诱惑,引诱
　　　attract 引起注意,兴趣,乐趣

shelter
/'ʃeltə/

n. & v. 掩蔽处;掩蔽

As the storm burst, the crowds rustled to get under shelter.
当暴风雨来的时候,人们急忙躲避起来。

veil
/veil/

n. 面纱

Her face was covered in a white veil.
她脸上盖着白色的面纱。

perpetual
/pə'petʃuəl/

adj. 永久的

Don't make yourself a perpetual nuisance.
不要弄得自己老是惹人讨厌。

同 permanent

反 temporary

neutral
/'njuːtrəl/

adj. 中立的；中性的
The arbitrator was absolutely neutral.
这仲裁人完全不偏不倚。
[同] impartial

---

perplexed
/pə'plekst/

adj. 困惑的，不知所措的
We were perplexed by the sudden change in his attitude towards us. 他对我们的态度突然变化，使我们深感不解。
[同] confused

---

persecution
/ˌpəːsiˈkjuːʃən/

n. 迫害
Many people fled abroad at the time of the persecution.
许多人在大迫害时期逃往国外。
[同] oppression

---

sheer
/ʃiə/

adj. 纯粹的；彻底的
He won his position by sheer ability.
他赢得地位全凭才干。
[同] absolute

---

withdraw
/wið'drɔː/

v. 收回，撤销
Our forces have been withdrawn from the dangerous area. 我们的部队撤离了危险地带。
[同] take back

---

shield
/ʃiːld/

n. & v. 防护物；庇护
These hills will shield off north winds and protect the orchards. 这些小山能挡住北风，保护果园。

提高词汇

飞跃词汇

vision
/'viʒən/

n. & vt. 视力；想象；看法

He has very little vision in the left eye.
他左眼的视力很弱。

短语　have visions of 幻想

eliminate
/i'limineit/

v. 消除

The government is trying to eliminate poverty.
政府尽力消除贫穷。

衍　elimination *n.*

同　get rid of

反　retain

fatigue
/fə'ti:g/

n. & v. 疲乏，疲劳

The patient fatigued easily. 病人容易疲劳。

同　tiredness

become of

后来变成，结局是

What will become of those refugees?
那些难民会落得什么结果呢？

implicit
/im'plisit/

adj. 暗示的

He is able enough to bring out the drama implicit
on this occasion. 他有能力把这种场合所固有的
戏剧性表达出来。.

同　implied

反　explicit

UNIT 11

基础词汇

climax
/'klaimæks/

n. 高潮,顶点

A visit with the Indian chief was the climax of his trip.
访问印第安酋长是这次旅行中最令他兴奋的事。

 summit

address
/ə'dres/

n. & vt. 地址;针对……而说

This easy-to-read guide is addressed to those who meet the qualifications. 这本容易读懂的手册是为那些够格的人准备的。

搭配 address oneself to 致力于;向……讲话

barrier
/'bæriə/

n. 阻碍,障阂

The country has set up trade barriers against imported goods. 这个国家已树立起贸易壁垒来对付进口商品。

 obstruction

climate
/'klaimit/

n. 气候

The climate of Africa did not agree with her.
她不适应非洲的气候。

delete
/di'li:t/

vt. 删除

The patient's high fever deleted most of his memories.
病人的高烧使他的记忆丧失殆尽。

衍 deletion *n.*

 eradicate

74

clue
/kluː/

n. 线索

I think we might find a clue to the mystery.
我想我们可能找到揭开这个奥秘的线索。

同 hint

短语 give a clue to sth. 提供线索

embody
/im'bɔdi/

vt. 包含;体现

Parts of the old treaty are embodied in the new one.
旧条约的部分内容已收入新条约。

同 include

fault
/fɔːlt/

n. 过错;缺点

I like him despite his faults.
虽然他有种种缺点,但我仍然喜欢他。

同 blemish

反 virtue

短语 find fault with 挑剔,批评
at fault 有过错

gesture
/'dʒestʃə/

n. & v. 手势,作手势

He gestured me to a chair.
他示意我在一把椅子上坐下。

personality
/ˌpəːsə'næliti/

n. 个性,人格

The environment shapes personality.
环境造就个性。

同 character

persist
/pə'sist/

vi. 坚持,持续

She persisted in reading the newspaper at the dinner table.
她非要边吃晚餐边看报不可。

搭配 persist in 坚持不懈

personnel
/ˌpəːsə'nel/

n. 人员,职员

The personnel of the company has been decreased.
公司的人员减少了。

---

shock
/ʃɔk/

n. & v. 震惊;震动

The shock of the blast shattered many windows.
许多窗户在爆炸中震碎了。

---

short
/ʃɔːt/

adj. 短的;矮的

She has her hair cut short. 她去剪了短头发。

搭配　run short of 缺少
短语　in short 总之

---

add
/æd/

v. 增加

She tasted her coffee,and then added more sugar.
她尝了口咖啡,接着又往里加了点糖。

搭配　add to 增加

---

reduce
/ri'djuːs/

vt. 减少

When stores have oversupply of goods,they will reduce price to encourage sales. 当商店商品供给过多时,他们会减价以鼓励销售。

---

adapt
/ə'dæpt/

vt. 使适应;改编

Some animals will modify their behavior to adapt to their environment. 有些动物要改变它们的行为以适应环境。

衍　adaptation *n.*
同　adjust
反　unfit
搭配　adapt to 适应

拓展词汇

embarrassing
/im'bærəsiŋ/

adj. 令人为难的

This is really an embarrassing situation.
这真是使人为难的处境。

衍 embarrassment *n.*

---

deliberately
/di'libərətli/

adv. 故意地

I think she hurt my feelings deliberately rather than by accident as she claimed. 我认为她是故意伤害我的感情，而不是如她所称是偶然。

衍 deliberation *n.*

同 on purpose

反 accidentally

搭配　deliberate on 仔细考虑

---

favorable
/'feivərəbl/

adj. 赞成的；有利的

I hope you will give favorable consideration to my suggestion. 我希望你考虑并赞同我的建议。

同 advantageous

反 unhelpful

---

lay off

v. 解雇

The firm had to lay off 100 men.
公司只得解雇100名工人。

---

marsh
/mɑːʃ/

n. 沼泽

It is a marsh plant. 这是一种沼泽植物。

同 swamp

---

occupation
/ˌɔkju'peiʃən/

n. 职业

He is a merchant by occupation. 他的职业是经商。

同 profession

Week②Day④

77

begin with

以……开始

This book begins with a tale of country life.
这本书以一个农村生活的故事开始。

shift
/ʃift/

n. & v. 移动;轮班

He shifted the chair closer to the bed.
他把椅子向床移近。

短语　make a shift 设法过活

term
/tə:m/

n. 学期;术语

Give the answer in terms of a percentage.
以百分数来回答这个问题。

搭配　in terms of 在……方面

substance
/'sʌbstəns/

n. 物质;实质

There is little substance in the report.
这份报告没有什么重要内容。

unlike
/'ʌn'laik/

adj. & prep. 不同的,不相似的

She's very unlike her mother.
她一点不像她母亲。

impose
/im'pəuz/

v. 把……强加于

He imposed on me his own ideas about the novel.
他把自己对这本小说的看法强加于我。

搭配　impose on 把……强加于(利用,欺骗)

nominate
/'nɔmineit/

vt. 提名

Citizens nominate John for Mayor.
市民提名约翰为市长候选人。

衍　nomination *n.*

rectify
/'rektifai/

vt. 矫正

The professor suggested rectifying a few points on my term paper. 教授建议我修改我学期论文的几个要点。

同 correct

---

reconcile
/'rekənsail/

vt. 使和解；调停

Since the couple could not reconcile their differences, they decided to get a divorce. 因为这对夫妻不能和解彼此的分歧，他们决定离婚。

衍 reconciliation *n.*

同 compromise

短语 be reconciled with 与……和解

---

tentative
/'tentətiv/

adj. 试验性的，暂定的

The arrangement is only tentative.
这一安排只不过是暂时的。

同 experimental

反 definite

witness
/'witnis/

n. & v. 证据，证明

He is a living witness to the success of the scheme.
他是这个计划取得成功的活见证。

同 proof

---

shiver
/'ʃivə/

vt. 颤抖

The leaves shivered in the breeze.
树叶在微风中颤动。

同 tremble

---

visual
/'viʒuəl/

adj. 视觉的

A good ad is a fortunate melding of visual pictures and words. 优秀的广告是图文的巧妙结合。

飞跃词汇

cling
/kliŋ/

vi. 紧贴;坚持(意见)

The frightened child clung to her mother.
受惊的小孩儿紧紧抱住她的母亲。

搭配 cling to 坚持,不愿放弃

imposing
/im'pəuziŋ/

adj. 使人难忘的,壮丽的

She made an imposing display of knowledge.
她显示出令人叹服的博识多闻。

衍 imposingly adv.

同 impressive

harness
/'hɑːnis/

vt. 利用(以产生能量等);控制

We can harness a river as a source of energy.
我们可以利用河水作为能源。

同 utilize

搭配 in harness with 与某人联手,密切合作

perspective
/pə'spektiv/

n. 景观;观点

A snow perspective spreads before us.
我们眼前展现了一副雪景。

短语 out of perspective 比例不当地

UNIT 12

clumsy
/'klʌmzi/

adj. 笨拙的
His rowboat was a clumsy affair made out of old boxes.
他的划艇是用旧箱板制成的粗糙东西。
同 awkward
反 adroit
辨析　clumsy 笨拙的,不灵便的
　　　awkward 体态举止不协调

base
/beis/

n. 底部;基础
We picnicked at the base of the mountain.
我们在山脚下野餐。

coast
/kəust/

n. 海岸
They live on the coast. 他们住在沿海地区。
同 seaside

code
/kəud/

n. & vt. 密码;编码
Have you coded this book?
你把这本书编号了吗?

emergency
/i'məːdʒənsi/

n. 紧急情况
He was able to meet the emergency.
他能应变。
同 urgency
短语　at a dire emergency 在非常紧急的时刻

基础词汇

persuade
/pə'sweid/

v. 说服，劝说

They persuaded me to go with them.
他们说服了我一起去。

衍 persuasion *n.*
搭配 persuade sb. to do 说服

feast
/fiːst/

n. & v. 盛宴；参加宴会

The poor starve while the rich feast.
穷人挨饿，富人大吃大喝。

同 banquet

harsh
/hɑːʃ/

adj. 粗糙的

This cloth is harsh to touch.
这块布料摸上去很毛糙。

同 coarse
反 smooth

physical
/'fizikəl/

adj. 身体的；物理的

It is a physical impossibility to be in two places at once.
同时身处两地在自然法则上是不可能的。

nonsense
/'nɔnsəns/

n. 胡说，废话

I want no more of your nonsense.
我不想再听你胡说了。

搭配 make a nonsense of 搅乱

phase
/feiz/

n. 阶段

He is going through a difficult phase.
他正经历着困难阶段。

短语 out of phase 不协调的

82

physician
/fi'ziʃən/

n. 医师

A physician is respectable.
医生是受人尊敬的。

show up

出席，露面

I waited for an hour but she didn't show up.
我等了一个钟头，但她没有露面。

unstable
/ˌʌn'steibl/

adj. 不牢固的，不稳定的

The tower proved to be unstable in a high wind.
那塔楼后来证明是经不起劲风的。

adhere to

坚持；遵守

If you want to set up a company, you must adhere to the regulation. 如果你想建立一家公司就必须遵守规章制度。

vivid
/'vivid/

adj. 生动的，逼真的

The actor gave a vivid performance as the mad king.
演员逼真地扮演了那个疯狂的国王。
 lively

adequate
/'ædikwət/

adj. 适当的，足够的

The quality of the product is quite adequate for local purposes. 这产品的质量可以充分满足当地的需求。
同 sufficient
搭配 be adequate for 足够的

adjacent
/ə'dʒeisənt/

adj. 邻近的,接近的

There is a music program adjacent to the news.
新闻广播前面(后面)是一档音乐节目。

同 neighboring

反 distant

搭配 adjacent to 邻近

---

delicate
/'delikət/

adj. 精巧的;得体的

I admired your delicate handling of the situation.
我很钦佩你这样巧妙地处理了这种局面。

衍 delicacy *n.*

同 exquisite

反 coarse

---

feasible
/'fiːzəbl/

adj. 可行的,切实可行的

This is a feasible plan. 这是可执行的计划。

同 practical

---

delivery
/di'livəri/

n. 递送

The supermarket stopped free home delivery.
超市停止了免费送货上门的服务。

---

impulse
/'impʌls/

n. 冲动

He is ruled by his impulses. 他受冲动支配。

短语 on impulse 冲动

---

get over

恢复;克服

Have you got over your cold? 你的感冒好了没有?

同 overcome

拓展词汇

lead to

导致

A bad cold can lead to pneumonia.
重伤风可能导致肺炎。

refer to

vt. 查阅；提到

Don't refer to this matter again, please.
请不要再提这件事了。

show off

炫耀；使显眼

The dark-colored frame shows off the painting well.
深色的画框把那幅画衬托得很醒目。

object to

反对，不赞成

My mother objects to cigar smoking.
我母亲反对吸雪茄。

venture
/'ventʃə/

v. 冒险；胆敢（谦语）

Does he venture to object? 他敢反对吗？

短语　Nothing ventured, nothing gained.
　　　不入虎穴，焉得虎子。

提高词汇

impress
/im'pres/

vt. 留下印象

He impressed me as an honest man.
他给我的印象是个老实人。

衍　impression *n.*

搭配　impress on 使铭记

提高词汇

occupy
/'ɔkjupai/

vt. 占据
My books occupy a lot of space.
我的书占了很多地方。
衍 occupation *n.*

shortage
/'ʃɔːtidʒ/

n. 不足，缺乏
There was no shortage of helpers. 不缺帮手。
同 inadequacy, insufficiency
反 abundance

break into

强行进入，闯入
Thieves broke into our apartment last night.
昨晚有几个贼闯进我们的公寓。

refine
/ri'fain/

vt. 精炼；使文雅高尚
He has refined his taste and manners.
他已经使自己的趣味爱好和举止仪态变得高雅完美。
同 polish

testify
/'testifai/

vi. 证实
The teacher testified to the boy's honesty.
老师证明那男孩很诚实。
同 verify

wizard
/'wizəd/

n. & adj. 魔术师；天才；极妙的
He is a wizard with horses.
他是个驯马行家。

turn up

出现
Let's not wait any longer, he might not turn up at all.
我们不要再等了，他可能不会来了。

飞跃词汇

embrace
/im'breis/

v. 拥抱

She embraced her son tenderly.
她温柔地拥抱儿子。

同 hug

marvel
/'mɑːvəl/

n. & v. 奇迹;觉得惊奇

I marvel at his rich imagination.
我对他丰富的想象力感到惊讶。

衍 marvelous *adj.*

同 wonder at

搭配　marvel at 感到惊讶

reference
/'refərəns/

n. 提及;参考书目

Keep your dictionary on your desk for easy reference.
把这本词典放在你的书桌上,以备随时查阅。

短语　with reference to 关于

coincidence
/kəu'insidəns/

n. 巧合;符合

It was no coincidence that the two disappeared on the same day. 两人在同一天失踪绝不是偶然的。

衍 coincide *v.*

短语　coincide with 相符

UNIT 13

be tired of

厌烦

I am tired of your stupid conversation.
你愚蠢的谈话我听厌烦了。

---

combat
/'kɔmbæt/

n. & v. 战斗,格斗

The ship combatted with the wind and waves.
船与风浪搏斗。

---

emphasize
/'emfəsaiz/

v. 强调

He emphasized the importance of being honest.
他强调诚实的重要性。

同 stress

反 underestimate

---

density
/'densiti/

n. 密度

This city has a population density of about 500 people per square mile. 这座城市的人口密度大约是每平方英里约500人。

---

fee
/fiː/

n. 费(会费、学费等)

Education fees are expensive nowadays.
如今的学费很贵。

---

feature
/'fiːtʃə/

n. 特色

The island's chief feature was its beauty.
这个岛的主要特色是风景秀丽。

同 characteristic

基础词汇

give up　　放弃

All hope of finding the missing plane was given up.
要找到那架失踪的飞机已毫无希望。

leak
/liːk/

n. 漏洞

The pipe has got a leak.
管子上有裂纹。

短语　A small leak will sink a great ship.
　　　小洞不补，大船吃苦。

mass
/mæs/

n. 大量；大批

Students gathered a mass of used clothing for flood
victims. 学生为洪水灾区的人们收集了许多旧衣服。

短语　be a mass of 充满，布满

planet
/ˈplænit/

n. (天)行星

We live on the planet. 我们生活在地球上。

reflect
/riˈflekt/

v. 反射，反映；反思

The moon shines with reflected light.
月亮是借反射阳光而发光的。

衍　reflection *n.*

短语　reflect on 深思

reform
/riˈfɔːm/

n. & v. 改革

He spent years trying to reform the world.
他花了多年的时间，力图改造世界。

基础词汇

until
/ən'til, ʌn'til/

prep. & conj. 到……为止
It was cold from November until April.
天气从11月份一直冷到4月。

---

word
/wɜːd/

n. 字,词
What does the word mean?
这个词是什么意思?
短语　word for word 逐字的

---

reflection
/ri'flekʃən/

n. 沉思;反映
This poem is a reflection of my mood at the time I wrote it. 这首诗抒发了我执笔当时的心情。
同　speculation

---

scale
/skeil/

n. 刻度;比例
This ruler has one scale in centimetres and another in inches. 这把尺上有厘米的刻度和英寸的刻度。
短语　out of scale 不成比例

拓展词汇

adjust
/ə'dʒʌst/

vt. 调整;使适合
The eyes need several minutes to adjust to the dimness.
需要花几分钟的时间使眼睛适应昏暗。
搭配　adjust oneself to 适应

---

administration
/əd,mini'streiʃən/

n. 管理,经营
He is experienced in city administration.
他在市政方面有经验。
衍　administer *vt.*

denial
/di'naiəl/

n. 否认，否定；谢绝，拒绝

For me, to do as you ask would be a denial of everything I stand for. 对我而言，按你的要求行事就是否定我们支持的一切。

衍 deny *vt.*

同 refusal

反 acceptance

emit
/i'mit/

vt. 发出；散发

Animal bodies emit perspiration.
动物身体会出汗。

衍 emission *n.*

hasty
/'heisti/

adj. 匆忙的，草率的

We should beware of making hasty decisions.
我们应谨防作出草率的决定。

衍 hastiness *n.*

occur
/ə'kəː/

vi. 发生；出现

When did the earthquake occur?
地震是什么时候发生的？

同 arise

pick up

捡起；获得

The bird picked up a worm.
鸟叼起虫子。

shrewd
/ʃruːd/

n. & adj. 精明的；精明

All you need is a lot of shrewd.
你需要的乃是机敏。

同 smart

反 stupid

拓展词汇

thankful
/'θæŋkfəl/

adj. 感谢的，感激的
There's a great deal for him to be thankful.
有许多事是他应该感恩的。

marvelous
/'mɑːvələs/

adj. 不可思议的；奇妙的
It is marvelous that we could see each other again after graduation four years ago. 毕业四年之后我们能再见面真是太美妙了。
同 wonderful

thanks to

由于，多亏
Thanks to the bad weather, the match had been cancelled.
多亏天气不好，比赛取消了。

提高词汇

administer
/əd'ministə/

v. 管理
In many Japanese homes, the funds are administered by the wife. 在许多日本家庭，钱是妻子掌管的。
同 manage

collide
/kə'laid/

vi. 碰撞
The car collided with the truck.
汽车和卡车相撞了。
搭配 collide with 相撞

collaboration
/kə,læbə'reiʃən/

n. 协作
The novel is a collaboration.
这部小说是协力创作的成果。
衍 collaborate *vt.*
同 cooperation
搭配 in collaboration with 与……合作

92

in response to

答复;反应

This remarkable girl was sent to me in response to my request for a suitable secretary. 他应我需要一名合格秘书的要求,给我派来这个出色的姑娘。

in honor of

向……表示敬意;为祝贺……

They held a banquet in honor of the delegation.
他们设宴招待代表团。

pierce
/piəs/

vt. 刺穿

The thorn pierced his heel.
那根刺刺入他的脚跟。

pinch
/pintʃ/

v. 捏,掐

The shoes pinch my toes. 我的鞋紧的夹脚趾。

短语　pinch and save 省吃俭用

shrug
/ʃrʌg/

v. 耸肩

She shrugged her shoulders at the news.
她听到这个消息后只是耸了耸肩。

verbal
/'vɜːbəl/

adj. 口头的

The difference is merely verbal.
差别仅仅在于措辞。

同　oral

反　written

come round

(怒气,争论等)平息

They often argue but it doesn't take them long to come round. 他们常常争吵,但很快就和好如初。

sieve
/siv/

n. 筛,滤网

You have a sieve of a memory.
你这人什么也记不住。

notation
/nəu'teiʃən/

n. 符号;乐谱

He made a notation on the margin of the paper.
他在纸的页边上作了批注。

shrink
/ʃriŋk/

v. 收缩

In our highly technological society, the number of jobs for unskilled workers is shrinking. 在我们这个高科技的社会，无技术工人的工作岗位正在减少。

同 dwindle

反 expand

UNIT 14

comfort
/ˈkʌmfət/

n. & vt. **安慰；舒适**
The nurse comforted the patient by tidying up his bed.
护士给病人整理床铺，使他躺得更舒服一些。
同 console
反 trouble

admit
/ədˈmit/

v. **容许；承认**
The little boy reluctantly admitted he had broken the expensive vase. 这个小男孩勉强承认是他打碎了那个昂贵的花瓶。
衍 admission *n.*
搭配　admit to 承认

enable
/iˈneibl/

vt. **使能够**
The eagle's large wings enable it to fly very fast.
鹰的巨大翅膀能使它飞得很快。
同 empower
搭配　enable sb. to do 使……能够

employment
/imˈplɔimənt/

n. **工作**
Finding employment nowadays is difficult.
现在找工作很难。
衍 employ *vt.*

fiction
/ˈfikʃən/

n. **小说**
I have read much detective fiction.
我看过很多侦探小说。

mastery
/'mɑːstəri/

n. 掌握

Man gradually achieved a great mastery over environment. 人类逐渐获得对环境更大的控制能力。

衍 master *vt.*

massive
/'mæsiv/

adj. 巨大的；雄伟的

Beethoven's Ninth Symphony is a massive work.
贝多芬的第九交响曲是气势磅礴的作品。

同 large

反 tiny

pleasure
/'pleʒə/

n. 乐趣

It's a pleasure to teach her. 教她真是件乐事。

notice
/'nəutis/

n. & v. 通知；注意

The matter attracted little notice.
这件事没有引起注意。

短语 come to sb's notice 引起某人的注意

refusal
/ri'fjuːzəl/

n. 拒绝，推却

They offered to buy his farm but met a flat refusal.
他们出价要买他的农场，但遭到断然拒绝。

衍 refuse *v.*

同 acceptance

sign
/sain/

n. 标记，符号

I saw him making signs at us.
我看见他向我们做手势。

同 mark

短语 sign in 签到

similarity
/ˌsimi'læriti/

n. **类似，类似处**

There is a great similarity among all her children.

她的孩子们长得都很像。

同 resemblance

反 difference

though
/ðəu, ðə/

adv. & conj. **虽然**

Poor though she is, her life is happy.

她尽管穷，但生活很幸福。

短语 as though 好像

signal
/'signl/

n. **信号**

The train stopped at the red signal.

列车遇红灯而停车。

plentiful
/'plentifəl/

adj. **大量的**

The deer are plentiful here. 这一带鹿很多。

同 abundant

反 scant

admission
/əd'miʃən/

n. **允许进入**

The ticket will give you free admission to the exhibition.

有了这张票，你可以免费参观游览。

短语 gain admission to 准许进入

admiration
/ˌædmə'reiʃən/

n. **欣赏**

The tourists paused in admiration of the beautiful view.

游客驻足观赏这美丽的景色。

同 worship

反 contempt

拓展词汇

beam
/biːm/

v. 放出束状的光(或热)

I beamed my flashlight into the corner and saw a mouse.
我把手电筒照向墙角,看见一只老鼠。

come up with

提出

He could always come up with a reason for them to linger another month. 他总能想出理由来让他们再待上一个月。

deposit
/di'pɔzit/

n. 沉淀物

A fine soil was deposited by winds carrying desert dust.
风把沙漠的沙吹起来,堆积成一片细沙土。

短语　on deposit 储存着

commence
/kə'mens/

v. 开始,着手

The play will commence at eight o'clock.
戏将在8点开演。

 start

enclosure
/in'kləuʒə/

n. 围栏

There's a special enclosure where you can look at the horses before the race starts. 这里有一处特备的围场,在比赛之前可以先看看马。

in terms of

在……方面

Young people's attraction to stereos cannot be explained only in terms of familiarity with technology. 年轻人对立体音响的喜爱不能仅从熟悉技术的角度来解释。

give up

放弃（念头、希望等）

He gave up his seat on the bus to an old woman.
在公共汽车上他把座位让给一位老大娘。

in spite of

不管

In spite of what you say, I still believe he is honest.
不管你怎么说，我还是相信他是诚实的。

thereafter
/ˌðeərˈɑːftə/

adv. 从那时以后

He was very ill as a child and was considered delicate
thereafter. 他幼年多病，其后一向被认为弱不禁风。

urge
/əːdʒ/

v. 催促，力劝

She urged that I should support the girls.
她恳求我支持姑娘们。

搭配　urge sb. to 怂恿，激励

work out

设计出

They worked out their own road to socialism. 他们开辟
了一条带有自己特色的通向社会主义的道路。

feeble
/ˈfiːbl/

adj. 虚弱的

His pulse is very feeble. 他的脉搏衰弱无力。

同　weak

反　strong

haul
/hɔːl/

n. & v. 用力拖拉；紧拉

The rope stood up under the strain of the haul.
这绳子经受住了紧拉。

同　pull

lean
/liːn/

v. 倾斜

He leaned into icy wind.
他弓着身子走进寒风之中。

短语　lean on 靠在,倚在

offend
/ə'fend/

v. 冒犯

His behavior offended against the rules of good manners.
他的行为违背了礼貌原则。

同　annoy

反　please

plead
/pliːd/

v. 恳求

She pleaded with me to give up the plan.
她求我放弃这个计划。

pledge
/pledʒ/

n. 保证,誓言

Esenhower fulfilled his election pledge to end the war in Korea. 艾森豪威尔履行了其结束朝鲜战争的竞选承诺。

verdict
/'vəːdikt/

n. 判断性意见

The critics may have hated the film, but the popular verdict was favorable. 评论家们也许仇视这部影片,但公众舆论支持它。

refreshment
/ri'freʃmənt/

n. 精力恢复

Would you like the refreshment of a hot bath?
你要不要洗个热水澡恢复一下精神?

衍　refresh *vt.*

飞跃词汇

depict
/di'pikt/

vt. 描述，描写

The painter tried to depict the splendour of the sunset.
画家试图描绘出日落的壮丽景象。

衍 depiction *n.*

同 describe

refrain
/ri'frein/

vi. 节制；克制；避免

Please refrain from smoking. 请勿吸烟。

反 indulge

搭配 refrain from 忍住，节制

辨析 refrain 忍住，克制
     restrict 限制
     constrain 被迫抑制

sight
/sait/

n. 视力，视觉

He had his sight treated by a doctor.
他让医生给他检查了视力。

短语 in sight 能看到

commemorate
/kə'meməreit/

vt. 纪念

The monument commemorates our victory.
这座碑是纪念我们胜利的。

衍 commemoration *n.*

同 memorialize

Week 2 Day 7

UNIT 15

adopt
/ə'dɔpt/

vt. 采用；收养

Congress adopted the new measures.
国会通过了新措施。

衍 adoption *n.*

advocate
/'ædvəkət/

vt. 提倡，鼓吹

The economist advocates abandoning the humanitarian and egalitarian goals. 这位经济学家提倡放弃人道主义和平均主义的目标。

衍 advocation *n.*

同 uphold

反 oppose

depression
/di'preʃən/

n. 沮丧；消沉

The Great Depression took place in 1930s.
经济大萧条发生在20世纪30年代。

衍 depress *vt.*

同 gloom

反 joy

短语 fall into a（deep）depression 变的抑郁

communication
/kə,mju:ni'keiʃn/

n. 通讯

All communication with the north was stopped by snowstorms. 北部的所有交通联系被暴风雪所中断。

搭配 be in communication with 与……联系

基础词汇

encouragement
/in'kʌridʒmənt/

n. 鼓励

The latest survey offers no encouragement.
最近的调查结果并不令人满意。

衍 encourage *vt.*

matter
/'mætə/

n. 物质

The entire universe is made of different kinds of matter.
整个宇宙是由不同的物质构成的。

同 substance

短语 as a matter of fact 事实上

mate
/meit/

n. & vi. 配偶

Birds mate in the spring. 鸟在春天交尾。

plunge
/plʌndʒ/

v. 跳进，投入

He ran to the edge of the swimming pool and plunged in.
他奔到游泳池边，一纵身跳进水里。

搭配 plunge into 插入，刺进

offer
/'ɔfə/

v. 提供

He was offered a job in Paris.
有人给他一份在巴黎的工作。

同 provide

搭配 offer to 提议；主动提出

短语 on offer 供出售的

regain
/ri'gein/

v. 收回，恢复

The army has regained the city.
军队收复了这座城市。

thread
/θred/

n. 线，细丝

Her voice is now a thin thread.
她现在说话的声音已非常微弱。

threaten
/'θretn/

vt. 恐吓，威胁

He threatened me with a gun.
他用枪威胁我。

衍 threat *n.*

worth
/wəːθ/

prep. & adj. 相当……价值

The place is worth a visit. 这地方值得一去。

搭配 be worth doing 值得

adore
/ə'dɔː/

v. 爱慕

People adore him for his noble character.
人们因他的高尚品质而敬爱他。

衍 adoration *n.*

同 idolize

反 dislike

plot
/plɔt/

n. 情节

How does the plot run?
情节如何发展?

sketch
/sketʃ/

n. & v. 素描；画草图

She sketched a hurried sign of the cross over her breast.
她草草地在胸前划了个十字。

拓展词汇

commonplace
/'kɔmənpleis/

n. & adj. 平凡的事

Jet travel is now a commonplace.
现在乘喷气式飞机旅行是很平常的事情。

同 ordinary

反 extraordinary

behalf
/bi'hɑ:f/

n. 利益;为了……

She laid a wreath at the Martyr's Memorial on behalf of all mothers. 她代表所有母亲在烈士纪念碑前敬献花圈。

短语 on behalf of 代表

commodity
/kə'mɔditi/

n. 日用品

The commodity boom departed nearly as quickly as it arrived. 商品繁荣来得快去得也快。

同 goods

deprive
/di'praiv/

vt. 剥夺,使丧失

He was deprived of his sight by the accident.
那次事故使他丧失了视力。

搭配 deprive sb. of... 剥夺

fierce
/fiəs/

adj. 凶猛的;猛烈的

He arrived with fierce pride.
他的举止表现出强烈的自尊。

同 cruel

反 tame

in the way

妨碍人的

If you are not going to help, at least don't get in the way!
如果你不愿帮忙,至少别妨碍人家!

given
/'givn/

adj. 特定的

The work must be done within the given time.
工作必须在规定时间内完成。

---

lease
/liːs/

n. 租约

Do you understand all the terms of the lease?
你明白租约的所有条款吗?

同 rent

---

poke
/pəuk/

v. 刺,戳

He poked me with his umbrella. 他用伞捅我。

搭配 poke at 拨弄

---

regard
/ri'gɑːd/

n. & vt. 关心,注意

I regarded the matter in this light.
我以这样的观点看待这件事。

搭配 regard...as 把……看作
短语 as regards 关于,至于

---

urgent
/'əːdʒənt/

adj. 急迫的,紧急的

There's an urgent telegram for you.
你有一份急电。

衍 urgency *n.*

---

figure out

计算出;明白

Does she have the adequate imagination to figure out
what happened? 她是否具有足够的想象力能猜出
发生了什么事?

---

in the light of

根据

He made his decision in the light of recent developments.
他根据最近的事态发展做出了决定。

提高词汇

notion
/'nəuʃən/

n. 概念

Her notion of rural life is a lot of sunshine and fun.
她心目中的农村生活是一片阳光和欢乐。

同 idea

poise
/pɔiz/

n. 姿势；镇静

She showed great poise during that difficult time.
她在困难时刻显得非常泰然。

simulate
/'simjuleit/

vt. 模拟，模仿

This kind of insect can simulate the dead leave.
这种昆虫酷似枯叶。

同 imitate

skeptical
/'skeptikəl/

adj. 怀疑性的

He listened to me with a skeptical expression.
他以怀疑的神情听我说。

同 suspicious

simultaneously
/ˌsiməl'teiniəsli/

adv. 同时地

In the past ten years, skyscrapers have developed simultaneously in Chicago and New York City.
过去十年摩天大楼在芝加哥和纽约同时兴建。

同 at the same time

verge
/vəːdʒ/

n. 边缘

It's illegal to drive on the grass verge.
在植草的路边驾车是违法的。

短语 on the verge of 接近于，濒于

commitment
/kə'mitmənt/

n. 许诺；承担义务

They held us to our commitment.

他们坚持要我们履行自己的保证。

encounter
/in'kauntə/

vt. 遇到

I encountered an old friend in the theatre.

我在戏院里偶然碰到一位老朋友。

同 meet

endeavor
/in'devə/

n. 努力

Please make every endeavor to come early.

请尽量早一点来。

同 effort

短语 do one's endeavor 竭尽全力

hazard
/'hæzəd/

n. 危险

Smoking is a serious health hazard.

吸烟严重危及健康。

同 danger

反 safety

辨析 hazard 偶然的或无力控制的危险

risk 自愿进行某种活动而冒的危险

threat 恐吓，威胁

短语 at hazard 在危险中

refute
/ri'fju:t/

vt. 驳倒，反驳

The argument can not be refuted at the moment.

眼下还不能驳倒这个论点。

衍 refutation *n.*

同 negate

反 confirm

UNIT 16

bend
/bend/

v. 弯曲

He bent the can opener.
他把开罐器弄弯了。
搭配　bend on 专注于

claim
/kleim/

vt. (根据权利提出)要求

Has anyone claimed the watch?
有人认领这块表吗?
同　demand

endure
/in'djuə/

v. 耐久, 忍耐

She can not endure to see animals cruelly treated.
她不忍眼看动物遭受虐待。
衍　endurance *n.*
同　bear

deputy
/'depjuti/

n. 代理人

He will be my deputy while I am away.
我不在的时候工作将由他代理。
同　agent

energetic
/ˌenə'dʒetik/

adj. 精力充沛的

Cool autumn days make us feel energetic.
凉爽的秋日使我们精神抖擞。
同　vigorous
反　feeble

109

mature
/mə'tjuə/

adj. & v. 成熟的；使成熟

Boys mature more slowly than girls.
男孩比女孩发育成熟的慢些。

同 mellow

---

finally
/'fainəli/

adv. 最后，终于

They finally finished their homework.
他们最终做完了家庭作业。

同 at last

---

glare
/gleə/

n. & v. 闪耀

These colors glare. 这些颜色太显眼。

搭配 glare at 盯着

---

polish
/'pɔliʃ/

v. 擦亮

This table-top polishes up nicely.
这个桌面能擦得很亮。

---

legal
/'li:gəl/

adj. 法律的；法定的

The manager is the legal person of the company.
经理是这个公司的法人。

同 legitimate

---

mean
/mi:n/

adj. & v. 低劣的，卑鄙的；意味

What does that sentence mean?
那个句子是什么意思？

基础词汇

slaughter
/'slɔːtə/

vt. 屠宰,残杀

Timber was slaughtered. 树木被砍尽伐绝了。

同 kill

porcelain
/'pɔːsəlin/

n. 瓷器

There is a valuable collection of antique porcelain in the museum. 博物馆里有一批珍贵的古代瓷器收藏品。

regret
/ri'gret/

v. 遗憾;悔恨

I regret my mistake.
我为自己所犯错误感到懊悔。

搭配 regret doing 后悔做过某事

slender
/'slendə/

adj. 苗条的

She was slender and had long dark hair.
她身材苗条,头发又黑又长。

同 slim

反 plump

compel
/kəm'pel/

vt. 强迫

The man felt compelled to talk to him.
那个人觉得同他谈话是被迫的。

同 oblige

搭配 compel to do 强迫

拓展词汇

affair
/ə'feə/

n. 事务

The party was a vast and lavish affair.
宴会规模很大,办得很豪华。

111

affection
/ə'fekʃən/

n. 喜爱

I have a great affection for him. 我很喜欢他。

同 fondness

反 dislike

搭配 have an affection for 喜欢;深爱着

endow
/in'dau/

v. 捐赠;赋予

John endowed a bed in a hospital.

约翰在医院捐赠了一个床位。

同 bestow

反 deprive

搭配 be endowed with (常用被动态)赋予

compensation
/kɔmpen'seiʃən/

n. 补偿,赔偿

He was paid a sum of money as a compensation for his loss in the fire. 他得到一笔火灾损失的赔偿费。

搭配 in compensation for 补偿

file
/fail/

n. 文件,档案

We have a file on every new criminal.

我们对每个新的罪犯都有档案。

短语 on file 存档

in vain

徒然

All our work was in vain.

我们白干了一场。

pirate
/'paiərət/

n. 海盗

Do you know there were many pirates in ancient years here? 这个地方在古代有许多海盗,你知道吗?

slice
/slais/

n. & v. 薄片,切片

Potatoes slice well. 土豆容易切片。

搭配　a slice of 一片

regardless of

不管,不顾

I'm buying the book, regardless of the cost.

我打算买下那本书,不管什么价钱。

register
/'redʒistə/

n. & v. 登记

This class has a register of 25 students.

这个班级共有25名学生注册。

skim
/skim/

v. 浏览

They just skimmed the headlines.

他们只浏览了一下大标题。

worthless
/'wə:θlis/

adj. 无价值的

Critics say his paintings are worthless.

批评家说他的画毫无价值。

in time

及时

Do you think we shall be in time to catch the train?

你看我们来得及赶上火车吗?

bring up

抚养

He has a big family to bring up.

他要养活一大家子人。

ponder
/'pɔndə/

v. 沉思，考虑
The prisoner pondered how to escape.
犯人细想如何逃跑。
同 think about
搭配 ponder on 沉思

---

thrill
/θril/

v. 使兴奋
The film thrilled the audience.
那部电影对观众很有刺激性。
衍 thrilling *adj.*
反 excite

---

threshold
/'θreʃhəuld/

n. 开始，开端
She opened the door and stepped across the threshold.
她打开门跨过门槛。
同 starting point
搭配 on the threshold of 开端，开始

---

verify
/'verifai/

vt. 查证，核实
The computer verified that the data was loaded correctly.
计算机已查实数据输入正确。
同 prove

---

affect
/ə'fekt/

vt. 影响
He was much affected by the sad news.
这不幸的消息使他大受震动。

---

filter
/'filtə/

v. 过滤，渗透
The news filtered through. 消息走漏了。
搭配 filter out 滤除

飞跃词汇

derive
/di'raiv/

v. 得自；起源

He derived his enthusiasm for literature from his father.
他对文学的爱好是受他父亲影响。

同 obtain

搭配 derive from 取得，得到

compact
/'kɔmpækt/

adj. & *v.* 紧凑的；使紧密结合

Racial and religious similarities compacted the tribes into a nation. 种族和宗教的相似之处使这些部落结合成了一个国家。

同 solid

notorious
/nəu'tɔːriəs/

adj. 声名狼藉的

His noisy parties made him notorious in the town.
他那些喧闹的宴会使他在镇上声名狼藉。

thrifty
/'θrifti/

adj. 节约的

She is a thrifty housekeeper.
她是个节俭的内当家。

同 frugal

反 wasteful

UNIT 17

benefit
/ 'benifit /

n. 利益,好处

The changes are to our benefit. 这些变革对我们有利。

同 profit

反 loss

搭配 for the benefit of 为了……的利益

describe
/ dis'kraib /

vt. 描述

Can you describe the accident in detail to me?
你能给我叙述事故的详细情形吗?

衍 description *n.*

同 portray

complain
/ kəm'plein /

v. 抱怨

They complained about being excluded form the
meeting. 他们因未能参加会议而抱怨。

衍 complaint *n.*

同 grumble

搭配 complain about 抱怨

engage
/ in'geidʒ /

v. (安排)雇佣(某人)

She was engaged as an interpreter. 她应聘当译员。

搭配 engage in 从事,参加

descend
/ di'send /

v. 下降

On turning the corner, we saw the road descending steeply.
拐弯的时候,我们看到路陡陡地下降。

搭配 descend from 起源于

基础词汇

Week③Day③

fit
/ fit /

adj. 合适的

It is fit to eat ?这东西也可以吃吗？

同 suitable

短语 fit on 试穿

financial
/ fai'nænʃəl /

adj. 财政的,金融的

There is a widespread belief that the company is in financial trouble.很多人认为该公司财务陷入困境。

同 economic

legend
/ 'ledʒənd /

n. 传说

He became a legend in his own time.

他成为他那个时代的传奇人物。

同 myth

measure
/ 'meʒə /

v.& n. 测量

Can you measure accurately? 你能量的准确些吗？

短语 beyond measure 无可估量

reject
/ ri'dʒekt /

vt. 拒绝

She rejected his offer of help.

她拒绝了他愿意相助的表示。

同 refuse

反 accept

position
/ pə'ziʃən /

n. 位置

The position of the house ensures a wonderful view of the coast.房子所在的位置让我们可以饱览海岸景色。

relate
/ ri'leit /

vt. 使联系

We are interested in what relates to ourselves.

我们关注与自己有关的事。

搭配 relate to 与……相关

slim
/ slim /

adj. 苗条的

Her waist was slim.她腰肢纤细。

同 slender

基础词汇

wound
/ wuːnd /

n. 创伤，伤口

The war has left deep psychological wounds .
战争给人们留下了严重的心理创伤。

辨析　wound 指外伤，也可喻指精神上的创伤
　　　injury 往往指意外伤害

competitive
/ kəm'petitiv /

adj. 竞争的

He doesn't like competitive sports.
他不喜欢竞技体育项目。

衍　competition *n.*

slip
/ slip /

v. 滑倒

She slipped and broke her leg.
她滑了一跤把腿摔断了。

拓展词汇

build up

增加，积聚

My savings are building up nicely.
我的积蓄增加得挺快。

after all

毕竟

The day turned out fine after all.
结果天还是转晴了。

competence
/ 'kɔmpətəns /

n. 能力

Her competence is beyond doubt. 她无疑是称职的。

衍　competent *adj.*
同　ability

in view of

考虑到，由于

In view of the recent developments, we don't think this step advisable. 由于最近事态的发展，我们认为这一步不可取。

means
/ miːnz /

n. 手段

All possible means have been adopted.
一切可能的方法都用上了。

短语　by means of 用，依靠

gleam
/ gliːm /

vi. 闪烁

His eyes gleamed with relief and joy.
他两眼露出宽慰和喜悦的光芒。

同　glimmer

heap
/ hiːp /

n. 堆

The building was reduced to a heap of rubble.
那建筑物已成了一片瓦砾。

同　pile
搭配　a heap of 一堆
短语　heaps of times 许多次

incentive
/ in'sentiv /

n. 动机

The fun of taking part in the game is a greater incentive than prize.参与游戏的乐趣比得奖更刺激。

同　stimulus

now that

既然

Now that they have taken matters into their hands, the pace of events has quickened. 他们既已着手自己来处理问题，事态进展也就加快了。

slight
/ slait /

adj. 轻微的，微小的

He had a slight headache.他稍微有点头痛。

throughout
/ θruː'aut /

prep. 遍及，贯穿

I could feel the tension throughout her body.
我能感觉到她全身的紧张。

passion
/ 'pæʃən /

n. 激情,热情

I hated them with passion. 我强烈憎恨他们。

同 obsession

enhance
/ in'hɑːns /

vt. 提高,增强

The Japanese scientists have found that scents enhance efficiency and reduce stress among office workers.
日本科学家发现香味能提高办公室工作人员的效率,并且能缓解压力。

衍 enhancement *n.*

同 elevate

反 degrade

porch
/ pɔːtʃ /

n. 门廊,走廊

The porch of this hotel is beautiful.
这个旅馆的走廊很漂亮。

portion
/ 'pɔːʃən /

n. 一部分,一份

A portion of the field was allotted to the sports club.
一部分田地划给了运动俱乐部。

搭配 a portion of 一份

reinforce
/ ˌriːin'fɔːs /

vt. 加强

This reinforces what you're saying.
这进一步证实了你正在说的话。

同 strengthen

反 weaken

thrive
/ θraiv /

v. 兴旺,繁荣

His business is thriving. 他的生意很兴隆。

同 prosper

反 wither

smash
/ smæʃ /

v. 打碎,粉碎

The ball smashed a window. 球打碎了一扇窗。

提高词汇

飞跃词汇

afford
/ ə'fɔːd /

vt. 供应得起
Can you afford a new coat? 你买得起一件新上衣吗?
搭配　afford to 担负得起

---

pose
/ pəuz /

v. 形成,引起
Beef exportation was greatly reduced because of the health threats posed by so-called "mad cow disease" in England. 在英格兰,由于所谓的"疯牛病"对健康造成了威胁,牛肉出口大大减少了。

---

complement
/ 'kɒmplimənt /

n. 补足物
Travel can be an exellent complement to one's education. 旅行极大地补充一个人的学识。
同 supplement

---

enforce
/ in'fɔːs /

vt. 执行
The principal enforced the rule of the school.
校长执行校规。
衍 enforcement *n.*
同 implement

---

offspring
/ 'ɒfspriŋ /

n. 子孙,后代
Their offspring are all very clever.
他们的子女都很聪明。
同 descendant

---

versatile
/ 'vəːsətail /

adj. 多才多艺的
He is a versatile painter. 他是多才多艺的画家。
同 resourceful

UNIT 18

aggressive
/ ə'gresiv /

adj. 好斗的,挑衅的
The unidentified disease made him aggressive.
查不出起因的疾病使他暴躁好斗。
同 forceful
反 friendly

bet
/ bet /

v. 打赌
I will bet a month's pay on that.
我愿意以一个月的工资就那件事情打赌。
同 gamble

design
/ di'zain /

v. 设计
The room is designed as a children's playroom.
这个房间设计成了孩子们的游戏室。
同 plan

deserve
/ di'zə:v /

vt. 应受,值得
She deserved first prize. 她应得一等奖。

despair
/ di'speə /

n. 绝望,失望
He was filled with despair by his failures.
由于多次失败,他完全绝望了。
反 hope
短语 in despair 绝望

flame
/ fleim /

n. 火焰
A flame of anger lighted in her heart. 她怒火中烧。
同 blaze

基础词汇

incidence
/ 'insidəns /

n. 发生

The incidence of murder that Sunday afternoon shocked the sleepy village. 那个星期天下午发生的凶杀案,震惊了这个一向沉寂的村庄。

flash
/ flæʃ /

v. 闪光

Lightning flashed in the sky. 天空电光闪闪。

heat
/ hiːt /

n.& v. 热,热度;加热

The fire doesn't give out much heat.
这个炉子的火不旺。

搭配　heat up 加剧;激化

post
/ pəust /

vt. 张贴

The results will be posted on the Internet.
结果将在互联网上公布。

incident
/ 'insidənt /

n. 事件

She told us about some of the amusing incidents of her holiday.她给我们讲了几件她假期中迫人发笑的事。

so
/ səu;sə /

conj. 因而,所以

Just as the French like their wine,so the English like their beer.就像法国人喜爱葡萄酒一样,英国人喜欢啤酒。

搭配　so as to 以便

relationship
/ ri'leiʃənʃip /

n. 关系,关联

What's the relationship of crime to poverty?
犯罪与贫穷有什么关系吗?

Week 3 Day 4

throw
/ θrəu /

v. 掷,扔

Stop throwing stones at the cars. 别再向汽车扔石头了。

短语　throw away 扔掉

wrap
/ ræp /

v. 包裹

A handkerchief was wrapped around his left hand.

他的左手用一块手绢包着。

短语　keep under wraps 保密

potential
/ pə'tenʃ(ə)l /

adj. 潜在的,可能的

That hole in the road is a potential danger.

路上的那个坑是个潜在的危险。

agenda
/ ə'dʒendə /

n. 议程

All such problems should be placed on our agenda.

所有这类问题都应提上我们的议事日程。

component
/ kəm'pəunənt /

n. 成分

Copper and Zinc are the components of brass.

铜和锌是黄铜的组成部分。

同　element

ensure
/ in'ʃuə /

v. 确保

His industry and ability will ensure his success.

他的勤劳和才能将保证他得到成功。

enrich
/ in'ritʃ /

vt. 使富足,使肥沃

The expanding economy enriched the peasants.

不断发展的经济使农民们富裕起来。

衍　enrichment *n.*

mechanism
/ 'mekənizəm /

n. 机械装置

An automobile engine is a complex mechanism.
汽车引擎是种复杂的机械装置。

care for

关心,照料

We must care for each other and help each other.
我们要互相关心,互相帮助。

omit
/ əu'mit /

vt. 省略

Minor points may be omitted.次要的可以删去。

postpone
/ pəust'pəun /

vt. 推迟

She knew that the day to perform the operation could not be long postponed. 她知道要做手术的那一天不能长期地推迟。

搭配　postpone doing 延迟

relevant
/ 'relivənt /

adj. 有关的

I don't think his remarks are relevant to our discussion.
我认为他的话和我们的议题不相关。

同　pertinent

反　irrelevant

搭配　be relevant to 与……相关

throw off

摆脱掉

The duck shakes its back to throw the water off.
鸭子一抖背部把水抖掉了。

carry on

进行,继续

Their conversation was carried on in English.
他们的谈话是用英语进行的。

complicated
/ 'kɔmplikeitid /

adj. 复杂的

The regulations are so complicated that they will only create confusion.规章制度如此复杂,只能引起混乱。

同 complex

反 simple

comply
/ kəm'plai /

vi. 顺从,遵守

We couldn't comply with your request.

我们无法满足你的要求。

搭配　comply with 遵从

enrollment
/ in'rəulmənt /

n. 登记,注册

His enrollment in the club adds much to its prestige.

他加入了这个俱乐部,使俱乐部的声望大增。

glimpse
/ glimps /

n. 一瞥

I caught a glimpse of her among the crowd before she disappeared from sight. 就在她消失在视线外之前,我在人群中瞥见了她。

搭配　catch a glimpse of 一瞥

call for

要求,需要

Success calls for hard work. 想要成功,必须苦干。

media
/ 'miːdiə /

n. 媒体

The media is often biased. 新闻媒介往往有偏见。

sober
/ 'səubə /

adj. 冷静的;未喝醉的

He is sober enough to drive the car.

他一点没醉,很清醒,可以开车。

同 cool-minded

提高词汇

飞跃词汇

soar
/ sɔː /

v. 高飞
His hopes soared.他的期望值提高了。
同 rise
反 plummet

release
/ ri'liːs /

vt. 释放
He released her hand.他放开她的手。

compliant
/ kəm'plaiənt /

adj. 顺从的
Department stores are compliant with the demands of custormers.百货商店依从顾客的要求。
同 obedient

nuisance
/ 'njuːsəns /

n. 讨厌的人或东西
Flies are a nuisance.苍蝇扰人。

smuggle
/ 'smʌgl /

vt. 走私
They smuggle Swiss watches in England.
他们走私瑞士表运进英国。
同 bootleg

verify
/ 'verifai /

v. 核查;证明
The bank will have to verify that you are the owner of the property. 银行必须核实你是该财产的所有者。

UNIT 19

agreement
/ ə'griːmənt /

n. 同意；协议

It will be very difficult to reach an agreement.
达成协议将是很困难的。

短语　arrive at an agreement 达成协议

between
/ bi'twiːn /

prep. 在……之间

The river runs between the two countries.
这条河在两国之间流过。

desperation
/ ˌdespə'reiʃən /

n. 绝望

In desperation, they resorted to violence.
在绝望中，他们采取暴力。

短语　drive sb. to desperation 逼得某人铤而走险

conceal
/ kən'siːl /

vt. 隐藏

He concealed a knife in his pocket.
我把小刀藏在衣袋里。

衍　concealment *n.*
同　hide
反　expose

despite
/dis'pait/

prep. 尽管

Despite a shortage of steel, industrial output has increased by five percent. 尽管钢材供应不足，工业产量仍增长5%。

pour
/ pɔː(r) /

v. 往……倒

He poured the wine into her glasses.
他往她的玻璃杯里倒酒。

短语　pour into 倒入

enthusiastic
/ in͵θjuːziˈæstik /

adj. 热心的，热情的

When we told him our suggestion, he was enthusiastic
for its immediate implementation.　当我们告诉他我们
的建议后，他很热心，想立即把它付诸实施。

衍 enthusiasm n.
同 eager
搭配　be enthusiastic about 热心于

heated
/ ˈhiːtid /

adj. 激昂的，兴奋的

John got heated with wine. 约翰喝了酒激动起来。

同 passionate

medium
/ ˈmiːdiəm /

n. 媒介

Air is a medium for sound. 空气是声音的传播媒介。

on
/ ɒn/

prep.& adv. 在……之上；（接触等）……上

She sat on the sofa. 她坐在沙发上。

reluctant
/ riˈlʌktənt /

adj. 勉强的

She gave a reluctant smile. 她勉强笑了一下。

同 unwilling
反 enthusiastic，willing
搭配　be reluctant to 不情愿

practical
/ 'præktikəl /

adj. 实际的，实践的

Earning a living is a practical matter.
谋生是个很实际的问题。

搭配 for all practical purposes 实际上

solution
/ sə'luːʃən /

n. 解答

The solutions to the question are at the back of the book.习题解答见书后。

thus
/ ðʌs /

adv. 因而，从而

Do it thus. 这样做。

practice
/ 'præktis /

n. 练习

Practice makes perfect. 熟能生巧。

destroy
/ dis'trɔi /

vt. 破坏，毁坏

He destroyed the painting. 他破坏了那幅画。

同 damage

alarm
/ ə'lɑːm /

n.& vt. 惊慌

They were alarmed to find her dead.
他们发现她死了，大惊失色。

短语 give the alarm 报警

enter for

报名参加

John entered for the examination.
约翰报名参加考试。

拓展词汇

entertain
/ ˌentə'tein /

v. 娱乐

The child was entertaining himself with his building blocks. 孩子在搭积木玩。

flatter
/ 'flætə /

vt. 奉承，阿谀

The music flatters her ears. 这音乐使人听得很惬意。

衍 flattery *n.*

同 compliment

短语 flatter oneself 自以为；自信

flaw
/ flɔː /

n. 缺点

Vanity is the great flaw in her character.
爱虚荣是她性格中最大的缺陷。

同 imperfection

incompatible
/ ˌinkəm'pætəbl /

adj. 不相容的

Those two people are incompatible. 那两个人合不来。

lest
/ lest /

conj. 惟恐

He ran away lest he should be seen.
他怕人家看见他而跑开了。

tick
/ tik /

v. 滴答

The clock ticked louder and louder in a quiet room.
钟的滴答声在静静的房间里变得越来越响。

nurture
/ 'nɜːtʃə /

vt. 养育；产生

Corruption nurtures resentment. 腐败滋生不满情绪。

同 foster

relieve
/ ri'li:v /

vt. 减轻

The tension was immediately relieved and the war scare was over. 紧张情绪立即解除了,对战争的恐惧已经过去。

短语 relieve oneself 排泄,方便

reliable
/ ri'laiəbl /

adj. 可靠的,可信赖的

This is a reliable pair of boots.
这是一双经久耐穿的靴子。

衍 reliability *n.*

同 dependable

aim
/ eim /

n.& v. 目标

His aim in life is to help the poor.
他的生活目标是帮助穷人。

同 goal

搭配 aim at 目的在于

短语 take aim 瞄准

compress
/ kəm'pres /

vt. 压缩,摘要叙述;(外科)敷布

Wood blocks may compress under pressure.
木头受压时会缩小。

同 condense

反 expand

inclusive
/ in'klu:siv /

adj. 包含的,包括的

The monthly rent is 150 dollors, inclusive of light and water. 每月租金150美元,包括水电费在内。

glitter
/ 'glitə /

v. 闪闪发光

A gilded temple glittered in the distance.
远处一座鎏金的庙宇闪闪发光。

短语 All that glitters is not gold.
闪闪发光物,未必尽黄金。

sole
/ səul /

adj. &. n. 单独的，唯一的；脚底，鞋底

She has the sole responsibility for bringing up the child.
她是唯一有责任抚养孩子的人。

同 only

solemn
/ 'sɔləm /

adj. 庄严的；严肃的

They made a solemn promise never to reveal the secret.
他们做出郑重保证，决不泄露秘密。

同 grave

反 light-hearted

precaution
/ pri'kɔːʃən /

n. 预防，防范

He was warned of the need for precaution.
别人提醒他必须注意防备。

wreck
/ rek /

n. 残骸

This ship was worthless wreck after a collision.
那艘船碰撞后便成了毫无价值的残骸。

compose
/ kəm'pəuz /

v. 组成；调解

The committee was evenly composed of men and women.
这个委员会由人数相等的男女组成。

搭配　be composed of 组成

compulsory
/ kəm'pʌlsəri /

adj. 强制的，义务的

In Scotland, compulsory schooling begins at age 5 and
ends at age 16. 苏格兰的义务教育从5岁开始，16岁
结束。

同 mandatory

反 voluntary

incorporate
/ inˈkɔːpəreit /

v. 合并，混合

He incorporated everyone's argument into his speech.
他把大家的观点融入自己的发言中。

衍 incorporation *n.*

同 integrate

搭配 incorporate into 吸收，纳入

mediate
/ ˈmiːdieit /

v. 仲裁，调停

America mediated between two warring countries.
美国在两个交战国之间进行斡旋。

衍 mediation *n.*

同 arbitrate

搭配 mediate in（between）调停

vessel
/ ˈvesl /

n. 船

This is an oceangoing vessel. 这是远洋轮船。

UNIT 20

concern
/ kən'sə:n /

vt. 涉及,关系到
The energy promblem concerns us all.
能源问题关系到我们每个人。

---

detect
/ di'tekt /

vt. 察觉,发觉
The teacher detects a flaw in an argument.
老师发现论点中有漏洞。

---

detail
/ 'di:teil /

n. 细节
No detail was overlooked. 没有忽视任何细节。
短语 go into detail 逐一说明

---

entry
/ 'entri /

n. 进入
At the president's entry, everyone fell silent.
总统一进来,大家就鸦雀无声了。

---

increasingly
/ in'kri:siŋli /

adv. 日益,愈加
China is increasingly prosperous and strong.
中国日益繁荣强盛。

envious
/ 'enviəs /

adj. 嫉妒的,羡慕的
I'm really envious of your new job.
我真的很羡慕你的新工作。
同 jealous
搭配 be envious of 嫉妒

flexible
/ 'fleksəbl /

adj. 灵活的,有弹性的

This job provides flexible working hours.
这份工作有弹性的工作时间。

同 elastic

反 rigid

---

heighten
/ 'haitn /

v. 提高,升高

Her make-up heightened her beauty. 她化妆后更美了。

同 elevate

---

melody
/ 'melədi /

n. 悦耳的音调

I love songs of soft melodies.
我喜欢旋律轻柔的音乐。

同 tune

---

remarkable
/ ri'maːkəbl /

adj. 非凡的,值得注意的

This painting is of remarkable quality. 这幅画是上乘之作。

同 distinguished

反 common

---

somewhat
/ 'sʌm(h)rwɔt /

adv. 稍微,有点

It is somewhat difficult to answer this question.
要回答这个问题有点儿困难。

---

to
/ tuː /

prep. 向,往

The industry today is nothing to what it once was.
这一行业的现状与昔日的盛况相比微不足道。

基础词汇

predict
/ pri'dikt /

v. 预报

The weather station predicts snow for tomorrow.
气象台预报明天会下雪。

同 prediction *n.*

反 foresee

space
/ speis /

n. 空间

There was just enough space for a bed and a table.
只有能放下一张床和一张桌子的地方。

remove
/ ri'muːv /

vt. 移开；除掉

They were removed from the English class.
他们已从英语班转走。

同 get rid of

反 retain

spacious
/ 'speiʃəs /

adj. 宽敞的

The topic is a spacious one, opening into many fields.
这个题目的范围很广，涉及许多领域。

同 roomy

反 crowded

alert
/ ə'ləːt /

adj. 提防的，警惕的

In our reading, we should always be alert for new usages. 我们在阅读过程中应该经常注意新用法。

同 watchful

短语 on alert 防备着

concise
/ kən'sais /

adj. 简明的，简练的

When answering questions, you should be concise and to the point. 你回答问题时要简明扼要。

同 succinct

反 wordy

bewilder
/ bi'wildə /

vt. 使迷惑

She was so bewildered that she did not know what to do.
她茫然不知所措。

衍 bewilderment *n.*

同 confuse

搭配 be bewildered by 使迷惑

allege
/ ə'ledʒ /

vt. 宣称，断言

The police alleged that the man was murdered.
警察声称那名男子是被人谋杀的。

衍 allegation *n.*

同 state

entitle
/ in'taitl /

vt. 给……权利（或资格）

The coupon entitles you to 10 dollars off your next purchase. 这张优惠券可让你在下次购物时少付10美元。

同 authorize

搭配 be entitled to sth. 给……权利

flee
/ fliː /

v. 逃跑

He should not flee from responsibility.
他不应该逃避责任。

同 evade

gloomy
/ 'gluːmi /

adj. 阴沉的

Their gloomy faces took away his appetite.
他们的愁容使他茶饭不香。

衍 gloom *n.*

同 depressed

反 delighted

let alone

不管，不打扰；别说；更别说

Let the poor little cat alone.
别去惹那只可怜的小猫。

predecessor
/ 'priːdisesə /

n. 前辈，前任

The advantage of Boeing 777 is that it is going to be a more efficient, wider, and technologically superior airplane than any of its predecessor. 波音777飞机的优势在于它要成为一种较之以前更有效，更宽敞，技术更出众的飞机。

同 forerunner

反 successor

remedy
/ 'remidi /

n. 治疗法

The remedy seems worse than the disease.
这种疗法比疾病本身更让人难受。

同 treatment

tidy up

整理，收拾

She tidied up the room. 她整理了房间。

alien
/ 'eiljən /

adj. 外国的，相异的

Luxury is alien to his nature. 奢侈与他的本性不容。

衍 alienation *n.*

同 foreign

搭配 (be) alien to 格格不入

conceive
/ kən'siːv /

v. 以为

In the past, the world was conceived of as flat.
过去人们认为地球是平的。

同 think of

deteriorate
/ di'tiəriəreit /

v. (使)恶化

His health deteriorated with age.
随着年龄的增长，他的健康越来越差。

衍 deterioration *n.*

同 degenerate

preclude
/ pri'klu:d /

vt. 排除

The adoption of one choice often precludes the use of the ther.选取了一种常常就不能用另一种了。

indicative of

预示的,可表示的

Her presence is indicative of her willingness to help.
她的出席表明她愿意帮忙。

meek
/ mi:k /

adj. 温顺的,谦恭的

She is as meek as a lamb. 她像羔羊般温顺。

同 mild
反 aggressive

opponent
/ ə'pəunənt /

n.& adj. 对手

He beats his opponent 3:0 他以3:0打败对手。

同 competitor

vibrant
/ 'vaibrənt /

adj. 充满生气的;活跃的

Thailand is at its most vibrant during the New Year celebrations. 在欢度新年的期间,泰国举国欢腾。

wretched
/ 'retʃid /

adj. 可怜的,悲惨的

His headache made him feel wretched.
他头疼得十分难受。

同 miserable
反 cheerful

alienate
/ 'eiljəneit /

vt. 疏远

The Prime Minister's policy alienated many back benchers. 首相的改革使许多后座议员开始对他持敌对态度。

衍 alienation *n.*
同 estrange
反 unite
搭配 alienate from 疏远

alleviate
/ ə'liːvieit /

vt. 使(痛苦等)易于忍受,减轻

His grief was alleviated by her sympathy.
她的同情减轻了他的悲痛。

衍 alleviation *n.*

同 relieve

反 worsen

incredible
/ in'kredəbɪ /

adj. 难以置信的

The plot of the book is incredible.
这本书的情节不可信。

同 unbelievable

concede
/ kən'siːd /

v. 承认

He conceded to the newsman that an immediate
agreement was nowhere in sight.他向记者们承认
近期无望达成协议。

同 admit

反 deny

UNIT 21

allow
/ ə'lau /

vt. 允许

He missed her more than he would allow himself to admit.他对她思念之深连他自己也不愿承认。

同 permit

反 prohibit

搭配 allow sb. to 允许

beyond
/ bi'jɔnd /

prep. 非……可及

Why does this excellent newspaper allow such an article to be printed is beyond me.为什么这份优秀的报纸要刊登这么一篇文章我实在是想不通。

wrist
/ rist /

n. 手腕

He has wrists of steel .

他有一副钢铁般强壮有力的手腕。

conduct
/ 'kɔndʌkt /

n.& v. 行为,操行;引导,管理

His conduct of the business was very successful.

他的商业经营很成功。

environment
/ in'vaiərənmənt /

n. 环境

He grew up in an environment of poverty.

他在贫穷的环境中长大。

衍 environmental *adj.*

glow
/ gləu /

n. 光亮,光辉

The glow of the setting sun is splendid; it is a pity that the dusk is fast approaching.夕阳无限好,只是近黄昏。

indifference
/ in'difərəns /

n. 漠不关心

She was much distressed by his indifference toward her.
他对她的冷漠态度使她深感苦恼。

同 apathy
反 passion

envy
/ 'envi /

n.& vt. 羡慕，嫉妒

She envied John for his success. 她妒忌约翰的成功。

同 jealousy

memorize
/ 'meməraiz /

vt. 记住，记忆

The child can memorize the alphabet.
这个孩子可以熟记字母表。

同 remember
反 forget

span
/ spæn /

n. 跨度；拃宽

She's still a hand's span shorter than her mother.
她比她妈妈矮一拃。

prefer
/ pri'fə: /

vt. 更喜欢，宁愿

Would you prefer tea or coffee?
你喜欢喝茶还是喝咖啡？

衍 preference *n.*

pregnancy
/ 'pregnənsi /

n. 怀孕

This is the seventh month of my sister's pregnancy.
这是我姐姐怀孕的第七个月。

衍 pregnant *adj.*

143

sparse
/ spɑːs /

adj. 稀少的，稀疏的

Vegetation becomes sparse higher up the mountain.
山上越高的地方植物越稀少。

同 scanty

反 plentiful

---

tolerant
/ 'tɔlərənt /

adj. 容忍的，宽恕的

She was tolerant of different views.
她能包容不同的见解。

衍 tolerance *n.*

反 intolerant

spare
/ speə /

adj. 多余的

We have no spare room for a table.
我们没有放桌子的地方。

prejudice
/ 'predʒudis /

n. & v. 偏见，成见；便……抱偏见

He has a prejudice against modern poetry.
他对现代诗抱有偏见。

搭配 prejudice against 偏见

短语 in one's spare time 业余时间

condense
/ kən'dens /

v. (使)浓缩，精简

Three months of meetings were condensed into just an hour.本来要开3个月的会议被压缩为1个小时。

同 compress

反 expand

---

repel
/ ri'pel /

vt. 击退

This kind of material can repel heat and moisture.
这种材料能够抗热防潮。

拓展词汇

allocate
/ 'æləukeit /

vt. 分派, 分配
A quarter of the total expenditure has been allocated to the public service. 经费总数的四分之一已拨给公用事业。
衍 allocation *n.*
同 assign

allowance
/ ə'lauəns /

n. 津贴, 补助
Each child has an allowance. 每个孩子均有零花钱。
同 allotment

fling
/ fliŋ /

vt. 投, 掷
He flung his books on the table. 他把书扔在桌上。

alter
/ 'ɔːltə /

v. 改变
The weather alters almost daily.
天气几乎一日一变。
同 change

heritage
/ 'heritidʒ /

n. 遗产
We must take care to perserve our national heritage.
我们必须注意保护自己的民族遗产。
同 inheritance

episode
/ 'episəud /

n. 连续剧的一集
This TV soap opera has 30 episodes.
这个电视连续剧有30集。

carry through

进行到底, 完成
We must carry the revolution through to the end.
我们必须把革命进行到底。

indignant
/ in'dignənt /

adj. 愤怒的,愤慨的

The actress was indignant at the reporter's personal questions.女演员对记者有关私生活的提问感到气愤。

同 furious

oppress
/ ə'pres /

v. 压抑

I feel oppressed by the heat. 我感到闷热难受。

衍 oppression *n.*

confess
/ kən'fes /

vi. 承认,坦白;忏悔

I must confess that I didn't understand a word she said.
我得承认我一点也没听懂她说的话。

衍 confession *n.*

同 admit

反 conceal

搭配 confess to 坦白

confer
/ kən'fəː /

v. 授予(称号、学位等)

The university conferred an honorary degree on him.
这所大学授予他名誉学位。

flip
/ flip /

v. 翻转;轻抛

He flipped to the next page and began to write.
他翻到另外一页,开始写了起来。

devastating
/ 'devəsteitiŋ /

adj. 破坏性的

To him, the criticism was quite devastating.
对他来说,那批评简直把人打得一蹶不振。

衍 devastation *n.*

同 destructive

UNIT
21

提高词汇

let down　　放下；使失望

Don't let me down, for I need your support.
别撇下我不管,我需要你的支持。

preface
/ 'prefis /

n. 序言；开始

The accident was the preface to a great scientific discovery. 这一偶然事件成了一项重大科学发现的先声。

sparkle
/ 'spɑːkl /

v. 发光,闪烁

Her eyes sparkled with excitement.
她目光闪烁,显露出激动的神情。

renovate
/ 'renəuveit /

vt. 革新；刷新

The church was renovated by a new ecumenical spirit.
教会因受全世界基督徒团结运动新精神的影响而恢复了活力。

衍 renovation *n.*

同 renew

deviate
/ 'diːvieit /

v. 背离,偏离

Nobody could deviate from the principle.
任何人不得违背原则。

衍 deviation *n.*

搭配　deviate from 背离

alliance
/ ə'laiəns /

n. 联盟,联合

The working class is in alliance with the peasantry.
工人阶级和农民阶级结成联盟。

同 coalition

飞跃词汇

Week③Day⑦

detrimental
/ ˌdetri'mentl /

adj. 有害的

A poor diet is detrimental to one's health.

饮食不良有害健康。

同 harmful

反 beneficial

搭配 be detrimental to 对……有害的

---

memorial
/ mə'mɔːriəl /

n. 纪念物

The statue is a memorial to a great statesman.

这尊雕像是纪念一位伟大的政治家的。

---

render
/ 'rendə /

v. 给予,提供;演奏

The piano solo was well rendered.

那支钢琴独奏曲弹得真好。

UNIT 22

confident
/ 'kɔnfidənt /

adj. 自信的，确信的

Are you confident of passing the entrance examination?
你有信心通过入学考试吗？

衍 confidence *n.*

同 self-assured

反 diffident

搭配 be confident of 确信的

equivalent
/ i'kwivələnt /

adj.& n. 相当的；等价物

This new refrigerator costs the equivalent of his whole year's salary.这个新冰箱的价格相当于他的一年的收入。

衍 equivalence *n.*

搭配 be equivalent to 相当于

ambitious
/ æm'biʃəs /

adj. 有雄心的，野心勃勃的

My brother is quite ambitious and plans to get an M.A. degree within one year.我哥哥非常有抱负，计划在一年内获得文学硕士学位。

衍 ambition *n.*

同 aspiring

反 undemanding

hesitate
/ 'heziteit /

v. 犹豫

I didn't hesitate to say it. 我毫不犹豫地把它讲了出来。

衍 hesitation *n.*

同 waver

149

dignity
/ 'digniti /

n. 尊严；高贵
The queen entered the room with great dignity.
王后仪态万方地走进房间。
同 nobleness

fluent
/ 'flu(:)ənt /

adj. 流利的，流畅的
He is fluent in English. 他英语掌握的很熟练。
衍 fluency *n.*

equip
/ i'kwip /

vt. 装备
He is equipped with a deep sense of justice.
他具有深切的正义感。
衍 equipment *n.*
搭配　be equipped with 装备

mend
/ mend /

v. 改进；修理
Crying will not mend matters. 哭泣于事无补。
同 repair

mention
/ 'menʃən /

v. 提及
Do not mention the accident before the children.
别在孩子面前谈起那事故。

individually
/ ˌindi'vidʒuəli/

adv. 个别地
I will speak individually to you later.
我等会儿单独跟你谈。

profit
/ 'prɔfit /

n. 利润，利益
They are only interested in a quick profit. 他们急功近利。
同 benefit
短语　make a profit 盈利

基础词汇

prepare
/ pri'peə /

v. 准备

He only had a few hours to prepare for the interview.
他只有几个小时为采访做准备。

衍 preparation n.
搭配 prepare for 准备

repetition
/ ˌrepi'tiʃən /

n. 重复

Let there be no repetition of this behavior.
别再干这种事了。

衍 repeat v.

torment
/ 'tɔːment /

n.& v. 痛苦；折磨

Stop tormenting that poor dog !
不要再戏弄那条可怜的狗了！

同 torture

concentrate on

专心于

He concentrated his attention on his work.
他把注意力集中在工作上。

replace
/ ri(ː)'pleis /

vt. 取代，替换

He replaced his brother as captain of the team.
他接替自己的兄弟出任队长。

衍 replacement n.

拓展词汇

epoch
/ 'iːpɔk /

n. 新纪元，时代

Einstein's theory marked a new epoch in the history of mankind. 爱因斯坦的理论标志着人类历史一个新时代的开始。

ambiguous
/ æm'bigjuəs /

a. 含糊不清的

The direction was so ambiguous that it was impossible to complete the assignment.指令如此模棱两可，以至于无法完成这项任务。

同 ambivalent
反 definite

close down

关闭,倒闭

The factory closed down for Christmas. 工厂停工过圣诞节。

---

go in for

从事

I thought of going in for teaching. 我想去当教师。

---

indispensable

/ ˌindi'spensəbl /

adj. 不可缺少的

Oxygen is indispensable to life.

氧气对生命是不可或缺的。

同 necessary

---

come about

发生

How did the accident come about?

事故是怎么发生的?

---

digest

/ dai'dʒest /

v. 消化

I can not digest my diner. 我饭后消化不良。

bid

/ bid /

v. 投标;命令;表示

Mourners gathered to bid farewell to the victims of the plane tragedy.哀悼者们聚在一起向空难者告别。

搭配　bid for 投标争取

compare to

把……比作

Shakespeare compared the world to a stage.

莎士比亚把世界比作一个舞台。

amplify

/ 'æmplifai /

vt. 放大,增强

Don't amplify the difficulties of the task.

不要夸大这个任务的困难。

同 expand

152

species
/ 'spiːʃiːz /或/ 'spiʃiz /

n. 种类,物种

There are more than two hundred and fifty species of shark. 鲨鱼种类达250种以上。

confirmation
/ ˌkɔnfə'meiʃən /

n. 证实

Enquiries failed to elicit either a confirmation or a denial of the rumor. 调查的结果既未能证实也未能否定这一谣传。

衍 confirm v.

dilemma
/ di'lemə /

n. 进退两难的局面

Two of my friends are having parties on the same day, and I'm in a real dilemma about which to go. 我的两个朋友在同一天举行晚会,该去参加哪一个让我实在难以决定。

同 predicament

短语 be in a dilemma 处于进退两难的境地

optimistic
/ ˌɔpti'mistik /

adj. 乐观的

She remains confident and optimistic, untroubled by our present problems. 她仍然信心十足,乐观向上,不被当前问题所困扰。

衍 optimism n.

反 pessimistic

搭配 be optimistic about 乐观的

specialize
/ 'speʃəlaiz /

vi. 专攻

Many girl students specialize in medicine. 许多女生专攻医科。

衍 specialization n.

同 major in

搭配 specialize in 专攻

提高词汇

prescription
/ pri'skrip∫ən /

n. 规定；处方

If you want this pain killer, you'll have to ask the doctor for prescription. 如果你想要这种止痛药，你得让医生开个处方。

衍 prescribe *v.*

toll
/ təul /

n. 代价；损失

The economic toll is heavy. 经济损失严重。

unprecedented
/ ʌn'presidentid /

adj. 空前的

The frankness of the interview was unprecedented. 会见的坦率实为罕见。

conceive of

想象，想到

I can hardly conceive of your doing such a thing. 我不能想象你会做这样的事。

confine
/ kən'fain /

vt. 限制

They succeeded in confining the fire to a small area. 我们成功地把火势控制在一个小的范围以内。

衍 confinement *n.*

同 restrict

搭配 be confined to 局限于

飞跃词汇

catch on to

理解，明了

Being a foreigner, Carl did not catch on to the joke. 因为卡尔是外国人，所以没有听懂那个笑话。

spectacular
/ spek'tækjulə(r) /

adj. 引人入胜的，壮观的

The spectacular dinosaur fossile can be seen in this museum. 那些最引人注目的恐龙化石可在这个博物馆中看到。

同 breathtaking

反 unimpressive

飞跃词汇

induce
/ in'djuːs /

vt. 劝诱，促使

Advertisements induce people to buy.

广告劝诱人们去购买物品。

衍 inducement *n.*

同 incite

搭配 induce sb. to do 引诱

confidential
/ kɔnfi'denʃəl /

adj. 秘密的，机密的；表示信任的

He spoke in a confidential tone.

他用信任的口吻说话。

同 secret

bitter
/ 'bitə /

adj. 苦的

The medicine left a bitter taste in the mouth.

药在嘴里留下了苦味。

同 acrid

反 sweet

UNIT 23

confront
/ kən'frʌnt /

vt. 使面临;对抗

We must confront the future with optimism.
我们必须乐观地面对未来。

短语　be confronted with 面临

spiral
/ 'spaiərəl /

adj.& n. 螺旋形的;螺旋

A coiled spring forms a spiral.
一条卷起来的弹簧形成了一个螺旋形。

contribute to

有助于,促进

Exercise and good sleep contribute to longevity.
体育锻炼和足够的睡眠有助于长寿。

annually
/ 'ænjuəli /

adv. 一年一次;每年

This medical journal comes out annually.
这种医学期刊一年发行一本。

衍　annual *adj.*
同　yearly

present
/ 'prezʌt /

n. 现在

He is a person who always lives in the present.
他这个人总是只顾眼前。

搭配　at present 现在

confrontation
/ ˌkɔnfrʌn'teiʃən /

n. 对抗,冲突

The president triggered a confrontation with Congress over the budget issue. 总统就预算问题引起了一场与国会的交锋。

基础词汇

Week④Day②

focus
/ 'fəukəs /

n. 焦点

She was the focus of everyone's attention.
她是大家注意的焦点。

同 center

搭配 focus on 关注于

---

preserve
/ pri'zə:v /

v. 保持

In case of emergency, he always preserves his calmness.
在紧急时刻，他总能保持镇静。

衍 preservation *n.*

---

dim
/ dim /

adj. 暗淡的；模糊的

He sat in a dim corner. 他坐在一个黑暗的角落里。

同 indistinct

---

ancient
/ 'einʃənt /

adj. 远古的，旧的

Many canals in our country were built by the ancient.
我国许多运河是由古人开浚的。

同 old

反 modern

---

erupt
/ i'rʌpt /

vi. 喷出；爆发

The volcano is due to erupt any day.
火山任何一天都有可能爆发。

衍 eruption *n.*

---

merely
/ 'miəli /

adv. 仅仅

I said it merely as a joke.
我只不过把它当作笑话说说而已。

diploma
/ di'pləumə /

n. 文凭,毕业证书

Mary gained a diploma in Applied Linguistics.
玛丽取得了应用语言学的学士学位。

---

reproduce
/ ˌriːprə'djuːs /

vt. 再生;复制

She tried to reproduce his accent.
她试图模仿他的口音。

---

split
/ split /

v. 劈开,(使)裂开

Let's split the chocolate bar among the three of us.
咱们三个把巧克力均分了吧。

gossip
/ 'gɔsip /

v.& n. 闲话,闲谈

Don't gossip about the neighbors' domestic problems,
it's none of your business. 不要闲聊别人的家务事,那
不管你的事。

同 rumor

conflict
/ 'kɔnflikt /

n. 斗争,冲突

The conflict berween Greece and Troy lasted ten years.
希腊和特洛伊之间的战争持续了10年之久。

同 dispute

反 accord

搭配　come into conflict with 与……不一致

dilute
/ dai'ljuːt /

v. 稀释

He diluted the paint with oil.他用汽油稀释油漆。

同 weaken

---

erase
/ i'reiz /

vt. 抹去,擦掉

Their ideal is to erase poverty and injustice from the
world.他们的梦想是消除贫困和不公正。

同 remove

flush

/ flʌʃ /

v. 奔流；晕红

Her cheeks flushed red. 她的双颊绯红。

---

reputation

/ ˌrepju'teiʃən /

n. 名誉，名声

He is winning a reputation among businessmen.

他在商界声名鹊起。

同 fame

---

cover up

掩藏，掩盖

Why do you try to cover up your mistakes?

你为什么要试图掩饰你的错误?

---

erroneous

/ i'rəuniəs /

adj. 错误的，不正确的

He received an erroneous impression.

他得到的是个错误的印象。

同 mistaken

反 correct

---

merciful

/ 'məːsifl /

adj. 仁慈的，慈悲的

Death came as a merciful release.

死亡成了幸运的解脱。

同 compassionate

反 cruel

---

preservation

/ ˌprezə(ː)'veiʃən /

n. 保存

This is a building worthy of preservation.

这是一座有保存价值的建筑。

同 conservation

---

rescue

/ 'reskjuː /

vt.& n. 援救，营救；援救，营救

Rescue was at hand. 救援近在咫尺。

同 salvation

短语 come to sb.'s rescue 救援

159

cut down

削减,删节
We must cut down our expenses somehow.
我们得想办法减少支出。

conform
/ kən'fɔːm /

vi. 使一致,使遵守
The new building conforms with the old-blend-ing-with-new character of the city.新大楼和该市新旧合璧的风格很匹配。
搭配　conform to 遵照

indulge
/ in'dʌldʒ /

v. 纵容
She indulges her son in whatever he wishes to eat.
她纵容儿子,他要吃什么就给他吃什么。
搭配　indulge in 沉浸于

liability
/ ˌlaiə'biləti /

n. 责任,义务
He has no liability in the matter; the liability is hers.
这件事他没有责任,责任在她。
同 responsibility

preside
/ pri'zaid /

v. 主持
Our headmaster will preside at our election of student union officers.我校校长将主持学生会干部的选举工作。
同 chair
短语　preside over 主持

spectrum
/ 'spektrəm /

n. 范围;系列
This exhibition covers the entire spectrum of space history. 这个展览会包括了宇宙空间从开始到现在的全部历史。

提高词汇

飞跃词汇

tow
/ təu /

n. 拖;拉

My car broke down but luckily someone gave me a tow. 我的车抛锚了,但幸亏有人让我把车挂在他车后拖行。

anonymous
/ ə'nɔniməs /

adj. 匿名的

He received an anonymous letter this morning. 他今天早上收到一封匿名信。

speculate
/ 'spekjuˌleit /

vi. 推测;思索

I can not speculate on their motives for doing this. 我猜不透他们这样干的目的是什么。

衍 speculation *n.*

搭配 speculate on 思索

analogy
/ ə'nælədʒi /

n. 类似

I see no analogy between your problem and mine. 我认为你我面临的问题并无相似之处。

inevitable
/ in'evitəbl /

adj. 不可避免的,必然的

The great speed of the car made the accident inevitable. 汽车开得这么快,使得那场车祸不可避免。

toxic
/ 'tɔksik /

adj. 有毒的,中毒的

When spilled into the sea , oil can be toxic to marine plants and animals. 石油溢入海洋可能危害海洋动植物。

同 poisonous

反 harmless

optimum
/ 'ɔptiməm /

n. 最佳效果

They are not functioning at their optimum. 他们并非在最有效的工作。

UNIT 24

blame
/ bleim /

n.& vt. 责备，谴责

Everyone threw the blame on me. 大家都归罪于我。

同 reproach

辨析　blame 责备
　　　accuse 控诉
　　　rebuke 谴责，非难

---

disappear
/ ˌdisə'piə /

vi. 消失

The dog disappeared into the night. 狗消失在夜色中。

衍 disapperance *n.*

同 vanish

---

follow
/ 'fɔləu /

v. 跟随，追随

July follows June. 六月过后是七月。

短语　as follows 如下

---

gradual
/ 'grædʒuəl /

adj. 逐渐的，逐步的

A child's growth into an adult is gradual.
儿童长大成人是个渐进的过程。

同 step by step

反 sudden

---

conquer
/ 'kɔŋkə /

vt. 征服，战胜

They vowed to fight and to conquer.
他们发誓要战而胜之。

衍 conquest *n.*

同 overcome

merge
/ məːdʒ /

v. 合并

John and Mary sought to merge their differences.
约翰和玛丽应试图消除他们间的分歧。

同 mix

反 separate

搭配 merge into 合并

essence
/ 'esns /

n. 本质

Being thoughtful of others is the essence of politeness.
体贴别人是礼貌的本质。

同 core

搭配 in essence 实质

consciousness
/ 'kɔnʃəsnis /

n. 意识；知觉

His consciousness of the urgency of the situation encouraged him to hurry up. 他意识到情况紧急，所以加快了脚步。

同 awareness

反 unconsciousness

applaud
/ ə'plɔːd /

v. 拍手喝彩，称赞

The president was applauded for his strong support of the bill. 总统由于强烈支持这一法案而受到赞扬。

衍 applause *n.*

同 praise

pressure
/ 'preʃə /

n. 压力

The pressure of the wind filled the sails of the boat.
风力使船帆张满。

同 tension

短语 under pressure 有压力

confusion
/ kən'fjuːʒən /

n. 混乱;混淆

I have some confusion about what the next step should be.对下一步该怎么做我还有些迷惑。

衍 confuse *v.*

同 bewilderment

反 clarity

辨析　confuse 混淆

　　　puzzle 迷惑,糊涂

　　　perplex 心情的困惑

discard
/ dis'kɑːd /

v. 丢弃,抛弃;放弃

Don't discard an old friend. 不要抛弃老朋友。

同 desert

anxiety
/ æŋ'zaiəti /

n. 忧虑,焦急

There was much anxiety about the future of these theatres.人们对这些剧院的前途忧心忡忡。

同 tension

反 relaxation

forbid
/ fə'bid /

v. 禁止

Parking Forbidden.禁止停车。

同 ban

搭配　forbid to do 禁止

traditional
/ trə'diʃn(ə)l /

adj. 传统的,惯例的

This is a traditional English breakfast .
这是传统的英国式早餐。

同 conventional

victim
/ 'viktim /

n. 受害人,牺牲者

He is a cancer victim. 他是癌症患者。

anticipate
/ æn'tisipeit /

vt. 预期，期望

You're always anticipating trouble.
你这人总是事情还没发生便往坏处想。

衍 anticipation *n.*

同 expect

conquest
/ 'kɔŋkwest /

n. 征服；战利品

He addressed himself to the conquest of women.
他成天忙于博得女人们的欢心。

infect
/ in'fekt /

vt. 传染，感染

Anyone with a bad cold may infect the people around him.任何重感冒患者都可能把病传染给周围的人。

衍 infection *n.*

搭配 be infected with 感染

infer
/ in'fəː /

v. 推断

From his grades, I inferred that he was a good student.
我根据他的成绩推测，他是个好学生。

衍 inference *n.*

同 deduce

liable
/ 'laiəbl /

adj. 有责任的，有义务的

Is a wife liable for her husband's debts?
妻子对丈夫的债务负法律责任吗？

同 liability *n.*

反 obliged

搭配 be liable to 有……倾向的

165

拓展词汇

appealing
/ ə'piːliŋ /

adj. 吸引人的

I have never managed to make house keeping appealing to my daughter.我从未能使管理家务这种事对我女儿具有吸引力。

衍 appeal *v.*

同 attractive

press
/ pres /

v. 压,按

The children pressed snow hard to make snowballs. 孩子们用力把雪捏成雪球。

appliance
/ ə'plaiəns /

n. 用具,器具

Vacuum cleaners,washing machines and refrigerators are household appliances.真空吸尘器,洗衣机和电冰箱都是家用设备。

reservation
/ ˌrezə'veiʃən /

n. 保留,(旅馆房间等)预定

Sorry,the hotel has no reservation under that name. 对不起,这个旅馆没有用这个名字预定的房间。

衍 reserve *v.*

merger
/ 'məːdʒə /

n. 合并,归并

One solution might be a merger with another large electronics firm. 一个解决办法可能是与另一家电子仪器公司合并。

spot
/ spɔt /

n. 污点;地点,场所

Every man has his weak spot. 人人都有弱点。

辨析　spot 户内外有限特定的地方
　　　site 位置,场所

短语　on the spot 当场

track down

追捕到

It took me a long half hour to track him down .
我足足花了半小时才把他找到。

optional
/ 'ɔpʃənl /

adj. 可选择的,随意的

He registered the optional coures on linguistics.
他选了语言学选修课。

同 elective

反 compulsory

resent
/ ri'zent /

v. 愤恨,怨恨

Kleider greatly resented his being tarred and feathered by recent business scandals.克莱德因为最近的商业丑闻而遭到严惩,对此他极为不满。

衍 resentful *adj.*

spoil
/ spɔil /

vt. 损坏;宠坏

During the first week of the diet,you can spoil yourself a little.节食的第一周你还可以吃点美味的东西。

同 ruin

spontaneous
/ spɔn'teiniəs /

adj. 自发的,自然产生的

Each presentation from the two subgroups was greeted by spontaneous applause.两个分队的每次发言都赢得了自发的掌声。

同 impromptu

反 prepared

prestige
/ pres'tiːʒ /

n. 声望,威望

The secretary enjoys high prestige in the company.
那个秘书在公司里威望很高。

167

提高词汇

飞跃词汇

spur
/ spə: /

v. 刺激,鞭策

The magnificent goal spurred the team on to victory.
他们那一球进得漂亮,鼓舞了全队的士气,从而取得胜利。

同 stimulate

反 damper

escort
/ i'skɔ:t /

n.& v. 护送;陪同(人员)

Her escort to the ball was my brother.
陪伴她去参加舞会的是我哥。

同 accompany

answer for

负责

He has to answer for the consequences.
他必须承担后果。

escalate
/ 'eskəleit /

v. 逐步升高,逐步增强

The demonstration has escalated into a large uprising.
示威游行已激化成为一场大规模的起义。

衍 escalation *n.*

highlight
/ 'hailait /

n.& vt. 最显著(重要)部分;强调

Three new talents highlighted the year.
本年度最引人注目的事是出现了三位新人才。

同 spotlight

resemble
/ ri'zembl /

vt. 像,类似

He resembles his father.他像他的父亲。

同 look like

presumably
/ pri'zju:məbli /

adv. 推测起来,大概

Presumably he won't see you, if you're leaving tomorrow. 如果你明天离开,他大概碰不见你了。

同 probably

168

UNIT 25

prevention
/ pri'venʃən /

n. 预防,防止

Education is the best way of prevention against social evils.教育是防止社会罪恶发生的最好方法。

discipline
/ 'disiplin /

n. 纪律;学科

All children need discipline. 每个孩子都需要训导。

blank
/ blæŋk /

adj.& n. 空白的;没有表情的;空白

His face is like a blank page.
他的脸像白纸一样,毫无表情。
同 empty
短语 in blank 留有空白待填写

blend
/ blend /

vt. 混合

The poem blends the separate ingredients into a unity.
这首诗把几个分开的组成部分联成一个整体。
同 mix
反 separate
搭配 blend in 融合

disclose
/ dis'kləuz /

vt. 揭露,透露

Most movie stars are not willing to disclose their true age.大多数电影明星不愿透露其真实年龄。
同 reveal
反 conceal

estimate
/ 'estimeit /

v. 估计

Nearly 1 million are estimated to be jobless.
估计有将近100万人失业。

同 evaluate

forecast
/ 'fɔːkɑːst /

vt. 预见，预测

According to the weather forecast, it will be sunny
tomorrow.天气预报说明天天晴。

同 anticipate

apply
/ ə'plai /

v. 申请；应用

They applied the rules to new members only.
他们仅对新会员实行这些规定。

搭配　apply to 适用于

foresee
/ fɔː'siː /

vt. 预见，预知

He foresees that things will go well.
他预知事情将来顺利。

同 predict

grasp
/ grɑːsp /

n. 抓住；掌握

We have in our grasp a truly glorious future.
我们把握住了一个真正辉煌的未来。

consent
/ kən'sent /

vi.& n. 同意，赞成

Her father would not consent to her going abroad.
她父亲不会同意她到外国去。

同 agree

license
/ 'laisns /

v. 许可

I am licensed to tell you that.
我得到许可去通知你此事。

order
/ ˈɔːdə /

n. 次序

He listed the items in order of importance.
他把各项按重要性列出。

短语　in order 井然有序

resident
/ ˈrezidənt /

n. 居民

He is a member of the local residents' association.
他是本地居民联合会成员。

appropriate
/ əˈprəupriət /

adj. 适当的

Plain, simple clothes are appropriate for school wear.
简朴的服装适合上学时穿。

同　proper
反　unsuitable

stable
/ ˈsteibl /

adj. & *n.* 稳定的；马厩

A young stable lad let out another horse, and stood waiting for the one which the smith had almost finished shoeing. 一位年轻的马车夫拉出了另一匹马，站在那里等那匹铁匠已经差不多钉好掌的马。

application
/ ˌæpliˈkeiʃən /

n. 申请；运用

Portugal made a formal application to join the EEC.
葡萄牙正式申请加入欧洲经济共同体。

衍　apply *v.*
同　utilization

delight in

喜爱

My father delights in telling stories about my childhood. 我父亲喜欢讲我童年的事。

consequence
/ ˈkɔnsikwəns /

n. 后果

Such a mistake would perhaps lead to disastrous consequences. 这样的错误可能会导致灾难性的后果。

同　outcome

essential
/ i'senʃəl /

adj. **本质的，实质的**
Discipline is essential in an army.军队必须有纪律。
同 indispensable
搭配 be essential to 必不可少的

mighty
/ 'maiti /

adj. **强大的，有力的**
She gave him a mighty thump.她狠狠地揍了他一下。
同 strong
反 feeble

inferior
/ in'fiəriə /

adj. **下等的，差的**
The shop assistant is honest. If she finds the goods are of inferior quality she will tell customers directly. 这个售货员很诚实，如果是质量不好的商品她会如实告诉顾客的。
衍 inferiority *n.*
反 superior
搭配 be inferior to 逊色于

approximately
/ ə'prɔksimətli /

adv. **近似地，大约**
What was said approximately equaled the facts.
谈判的情况接近于事实。

previous
/ 'pri:viəs /

adj. **在前的，早先的**
Have you ever had any previous experience, or is this kind of work new to you? 你以前有过这种经历吗？抑或者对你来说是新工作？

consequently
/ 'kɔnsikwəntli /

adv. **从而，因此**
The young man has never been to China.Consequently, he knows very little about it.这个青年从未到过中国，因此，他对中国知之甚少。
同 therefore

stab
/ stæb /

v. 刺，刺伤

Three of the victims were stabbed to death.
三名受害者被刺死。

---

resign
/ ri'zain /

v. 辞去（职务）

He resigned from his office.他辞职了。

同 quit

appreciation
/ əˌpriːʃiˈeiʃən /

n. 感谢，感激

He showed no appreciation of my advice.
他对我的劝告并不领情。

衍 appreciate *v.*

同 gratitude

反 disrespect

discharge
/ dis'tʃɑːdʒ /

v. 卸下；解雇

Several of the recruits were discharged from the army due to poor eyesight. 几个新兵因为眼睛近视被部队开除了。

同 release

---

prevalent
/ 'prevələnt /

adj. 普遍的，流行的

Cold is prevalent in the winter.感冒流行于冬季。

同 widespread

反 rare，uncommon

hinder
/ 'hində /

v. 阻碍

Bad weather hindered travel.
天气不好使旅行受到阻碍。

同 prevent

反 facilitate

influential
/ ˌinfluˈenʃəl /

adj. 有影响的，有势力的

He is a very influential man in the government.
他是政府中颇有影响的人物。

同 authoritative
反 unimportant

merit
/ ˈmerit /

n. 优点；价值

Her singing is totally without merit.
她的歌声糟糕极了。

infinite
/ ˈinfinit /

adj. 无限的

Man has infinite ingenuity.
人类有无穷无尽的创造力。

同 boundless
反 limited

stack
/ stæk /

n.& v. 堆，垛；堆起

The grain had gone mouldy in the stack.
垛里的谷子发霉了。

prevail
/ priˈveil /

v. 击败；盛行

Reason prevailed over emotion. 理智战胜了感情。

衍 prevailing *adj.*
同 win over

stagger
/ ˈstægə(r) /

v. 摇晃，蹒跚

The ship staggered. 船晃得厉害。

同 totter

esteem
/ i'sti:m /

vt.& n. 把……看作;尊敬

I esteem him for his honesty.
我因为他为人诚实而敬重他。

同 respect

反 belittle

---

reside
/ ri'zaid /

vi. 居住

Where are you residing now? 你现在住哪儿?

同 live

---

trample
/ 'træmpl /

v. 踩踏;蹂躏

More people were trampled to death than were actually killed by the fire. 被踩死的人多于实际被火烧死的人。

同 tread on

UNIT 26

blink
/ blɪŋk /

v. & n. 眨眼，闪亮
She blinked as the bright light shone on her.
当强光照着她时，她眨着眼睛。
同 sparkle
搭配 on the blink 坏了；需修理

---

principal
/ 'prɪnsəp(ə)l /

adj. 主要的，首要的
What's your principal reason for wanting to be a doctor?
你想当医生的主要原因是什么？
同 major

---

dismiss
/ dɪs'mɪs /

v. 解散；下课
The school was dismissed 15 minutes early. 提早15
分钟就放学了。
同 release

---

forgivable
/ 'fə'gɪvəbl /

adj. 可宽恕的
Telling lies are not forgivable.
撒谎是不可原谅的。

---

primitive
/ 'prɪmɪtɪv /

adj. 原始的，远古的
Primitive man made himself primitive tools from sharp
stones and animal bones. 原始人用尖利的石块和兽骨
为自己制作原始的工具。
衍 primitiveness *n.*
反 civilized

基础词汇

formerly
/ 'fɔ:məli /

adv. 从前，以前

Formerly this large town was a small village.
这座大镇以前是个小村庄。

同 previously

---

argument
/ 'ɑ:gjumənt /

n. 争论，辩论

We get into an argument about whether to go by sea or by air. 我们开始了一场关于乘船去还是乘飞机去的争论。

同 contention
反 agreement

---

hint
/ hint /

n. 暗示，提示

Can you give me some hints on how to do this job?
这工作怎么做，你能给我指点一下吗？

同 clue

---

ingredient
/ in'gri:diənt /

n. 成分；因素

Mental illness and detachment from society are the ingredients of suicide. 精神病及不合群是造成自杀的因素。

同 element

---

lift
/ lift /

v. 提；抬

Lift your foot up. 把你的脚抬一抬。

同 elevate
反 lower

---

ordinary
/ 'ɔ:dənri /

adj. 平常的，普通的

Her ordinary tone of voice is very loud.
她通常说话的声音很响。

同 common
反 unusual

primary
/ 'praiməri /

adj. 第一位的，主要的

A primary cause of his failure is his laziness.
懒惰是他失败的主要原因之一。

同 major

反 minor

resist
/ ri'zist /

vt. 抵抗，反抗

Lovers of night life won't be able to resist nightclubs in the area. 喜欢夜生活的人们不能抵抗该地区许多夜总会的诱惑。

同 oppose

反 yield

stain
/ stein /

n.& v. 污点

His shirt was stained. 他衬衫上沾有血迹。

同 taint

principle
/ 'prinsəpl /

n. 法则；原则

It's a principle of mine not to eat between meals.
两餐之间不要吃零食是我的一个准则。

同 belief

短语　in principle 原则上

transfer
/ træns'fəː /

v. 迁移；移动

They transferred 20 bags of jewels into a waiting car.
他们把20袋珠宝搬进一辆等着的汽车。

同 relocate

apt
/ æpt /

adj. 恰当的

"Love at first sight" is a very apt description of how John felt when he saw Mary. "一见钟情"是对约翰见到玛丽的一个恰当描述。

同 proper

搭配　be apt to 有……倾向的

transform
/ træns'fɔːm /

v. 转换，改变

A steam engine transforms heat into energy.
蒸汽把热量变成能量。

衍 transformation *n.*

同 change

disguise
/ dis'gaiz /

v.& n. 假装，伪装

He was disguised as a policeman. 他装扮成警察。

同 cover up

反 expose

短语 in disguise 伪装

conserve
/ kən'səːv /

vt. 保存；节省

He writes on both sides of the sheet to conserve paper.
他在纸张的两面都写以节省用纸。

衍 conservation *n.*

同 preserve

evaluate
/ i'væljueit /

v. 评价

How would you evaluate yourself ?
你将对自己如何评价？

衍 evaluation *n.*

同 estimate

conservative
/ kən'səːvətiv /

adj. 保守的，守旧的

Old people tend to be conservative in their attitudes.
老年人的看法往往保守。

同 traditional

反 progressive

拓展词汇

stale
/ steil /

adj. 不新鲜的,陈腐的

These old peanuts taste stale.这些陈花生变味了。

衍 staleness *n.*

反 fresh

even if

即使

I'll come even if it rains.即使天下雨我也会来。

considerate
/ kən'sidərit /

adj. 考虑周到的

It was very considerate of you to send me a birthday card.谢谢你给我寄来生日卡。

衍 considerateness *n.*

同 thoughtful

resort
/ ri'zɔːt /

vi.& n. 求助;常去之地

The park is one of his favorite resorts.

这个公园是他最喜欢去的地方之一。

搭配 resort to 求助于

resolve
/ ri'zɔlv /

n. 决心

Don' t shake your resolve when encountering difficulties.

遇到困难时不要动摇决心。

同 determination

arise
/ ə'raiz /

vi. 出现;发生

New problems arise daily.新问题每天产生。

同 emerge

提高词汇

greasy
/ 'griːsi /

adj. 油脂的

Greasy food is hard to digest.油腻食物难于消化。

180

blunder
/ 'blʌndə /

n. 大错；失误

A last-minute blunder cost them the match.
最后关头的错误让他们输掉了比赛。

同 error

辨析 blunder 大错
error 错误，过失
drawback 缺点，不足之处

短语 make a blunder 犯大错误

considerable
/ kən'sidərəbl /

adj. 相当大（多）的

I need a new designer and you need to find a way to get out of a considerable financial mess. 我需要一个新的设计师，你需要想办法跳出大的财务困境。

同 sizable

stake
/ steik /

n.& v. 树桩；打赌

He planted and staked all the new trees.
他新种了许多树并用树桩把他们撑好。

migrate
/ mai'greit /

vi. 随季节而移居

Swallow migrates in the winter. 燕子在冬天迁徙。

同 emigrate

militant
/ 'militənt /

adj. 好战的

She is a militant feminist.
她是个战斗性强的男女平等主义者。

同 combative

反 pacific

stall
/ stɔ:l /

n. 货摊

The town square is full of traders' stalls.
城镇的广场上摆满了生意人的货摊。

arbitrary
/ 'ɑːbitrəri /

adj. 任意的,武断的

Don't make an arbitrary choice. 不要随心所欲做选择。

同 random

inherent
/ in'hiərənt /

adj. 固有的,内在的

Parents should be aware of the inherent nature of their children.父母对儿女的素质应有清醒的认识。

同 innate

discount
/ 'diskaunt /

n.& v. 折扣;打折扣

That store does not discount at all.
那家铺子出售商品一概不打折扣。

短语 at a discount 打折扣

eternal
/ i'tə:nl /

adj. 永恒的,永存的

Since a circle has no beginning or end, the wedding ring is accepted as a symbol of eternal love. 由于指环没有起点和终点，所以结婚戒指成为永恒爱情的象征。

衍 eternity *n.*

同 permanent

反 transitory

inhibit
/ in'hibit /

v. 抑制,约束

Shyness inhibited him from speaking.
他因害羞而说不出话来。

同 repress

反 encourage

182

UNIT 27

event
/ i'vent /

n. 事件

Her new book was the intellectual event of the year.
她那部新书是当年知识界的大事。

短语 wise after the event 事后聪明的

startled
/ 'stɑːtld /

adj. 震惊的

She was startled to see him looking so ill.
看到他病得这么厉害，她感到很震惊。

同 surprised

consist
/ kən'sist /

vi. 由……组成；存在

The house consists of six rooms.
这幢房子由六个房间组成。

搭配   consist of 由……组成

standardize
/ 'stændədaiz /

vt. 使标准化

Standardized products are sold here.
这里出售的都是标准化的产品。

evident
/ 'evidənt /

adj. 明显的，显然的

It is evident that we do not understand each other.
显然，我们彼此不了解。

同 obvious

formidable
/ 'fɔːmidəbl /

adj. 令人敬畏的；可怕的

They climbed the last part of the mountain in formidable weather condition. 他们在恶劣的天气条件下爬上了山顶。

同 frightful

反 cheerful

基础词汇

consistent
/ kən'sistənt /

adj. 一致的

The professor has a consistent attitude towards all the students.这位教授对他所有的学生一视同仁。

同 compatible

反 contradictory

historical
/ hi'stɔrikəl /

adj. 历史(上)的

We have no historical evidence for it.
我们缺乏可以证明这一点的史学根据。

辨析　historic 有历史意义的
　　　　historical 历史上的(别于传说和虚构)

organize
/ 'ɔːgənaiz /

vt. 组织

The meeting was badly organized.会议组织地很糟糕。

衍 organization *n.*

同 arrange

反 disband

privacy
/ 'praivəsi /

n. 隐私

A person should have some privacy.
一个人总该有点自己的私生活。

衍 private *adj.*

同 secrecy

privilege
/ 'privilidʒ /

n. 特权

One of the obstacles to social harmony is privilege.
导致社会不和谐的障碍之一就是特权。

formulate
/ 'fɔːmjuleit /

vt. 用公式表示;明确地表达

The boss formulated a marketing plan for the next year.
老板制定了下个年度的营销计划。

resource
/ ri'sɔːs /

n. 资源

Oil is Kuwait's most important resource.
石油是科威特最重要的资源。

arrest
/ ə'rest /

vt. 逮捕

A man was arrested on suspicion of having murdered the girl.一个男人因有谋害少女的嫌疑而被捕。

stand
/ stænd /

v. 站立

I stood still . 我一动不动地站着。

短语　stand by 袖手旁观

transmission
/ trænz'miʃən /

n. 输送；传播

Cultural transmission indicates that human beings hand their languages down from one generation to another. 文化传播把人类的语言一代一代传下来。

衍 transmit *v.*

arouse
/ ə'rauz /

v. 唤醒

The noise aroused me from sleep.
吵闹声把我从睡梦中吵醒。

context
/ 'kɔntekst /

n. 上下文

To appreciate what these changes will mean, it is necessary to look at them in context.要想搞清楚这些变化意味着什么，有必要看一看他们所处的环境。

同 background

blunt
/ blʌnt /

adj. 钝的；率直的

To be blunt, I think that company has made a complete mess of everything. 坦率地讲，我认为那个公司把事情搞得一团糟。

Week 4 Day 6

disorder
/ dis'ɔːdə /

n. 混乱

The strike threw the whole country into disorder.
罢工使全国陷入混乱之中。

同 disarrangement

反 order

---

grief
/ grif /

n. 悲伤

She had to hide her grief. 她不得不掩饰自己的悲伤。

同 sorrow

反 joy

prior
/ 'praiə /

adj. 优先的;在前面的

Joe walked off his job without prior consultation.
乔未经事先商量就离开了工作岗位。

同 preceding

consolidate
/ kən'sɔlideit /

v. 巩固

They consolidated their gains by reinvesting in government bonds.他们通过再投资于公债而确保了收益。

同 strengthen

反 weaken

in the light of

鉴于,由于

He reviewed his decision in the light of recent developments. 他根据最近的事态发展重新考虑自己的决定。
Light come, light go.来的容易去的快。

miniature
/ 'miniətʃə(r) /

n. 缩图,缩影

The art of portrait miniature was originated in England.
绘制微型画像的艺术发源于英国。

短语 in miniature 小规模

transition
/ træn'ziʃən /

n. 转变;过渡

The transition from childhood to adulthood is always a critical time for everybody.从童年时代过渡到成年时代对每个人来说都是一个关键时刻。

衍 transitional *adj.*

同 transformation

initiate
/ i'niʃieit /

vt. 发起;使初步了解

She initiated him to the ballet.
她把芭蕾舞的基本技巧教给他。

同 originate

搭配 initiate sb. into sth. 把基础知识传授给某人

stand up to

勇敢地抵抗

A man who can stand up to such treatment is a man of remarkable physical strength and moral courage.
能够忍受这样待遇的人是具有非凡体力和道德勇气的人。

boast
/ bəust /

v. 自夸

I don't like John, for he is always boasting.
我不喜欢约翰,他老是自吹自擂。

同 brag

搭配 boast of 夸耀

disperse
/ di'spəːs /

v. (使)分散

He has ties with many widely dispersed friends.
他和他那些散居各地的朋友都有联系。

同 scatter

反 combine

evoke
/ i'vəuk /

vt. 唤起

The old film evoked memories of my childhood.
那部老电影唤起我对童年的回忆。

同 rouse

priority
/ prai'ɔriti /

n. 优先权

Fire engines and ambulances have priority over other traffic.消防车及救护车比其他车辆有优先通行权。

同 preference

短语 place priority on 优先考虑

artery
/ 'ɑːtəri /

n.& v. 动脉；要道

Great rivers artery every province.大河遍布各省。

mingle
/ 'miŋgl /

v. (使)混合

Although the colonists mingled to some extent with the native Americans, the Indians' influence on American culture and language was not extensive. 虽然殖民者与美洲土著人在某种程度上互相融合，但是印第安人对美国文化和语言的影响并不广泛。

同 intermingle

反 divide

respectable
/ ri'spektəbl /

adj. 值得尊敬的

It is not respectable to get drunk in the street.
在大街上喝得醉熏熏是有失体统的。

辨析 respectable 值得尊敬的
respectful 恭敬的

array
/ ə'rei /

n. 排列

The troops were formed in battle array.
军队按战斗队形排列。

提高词汇

dispatch
/ di'spætʃ /

vt. 派遣

Three engines were dispatched to combat the blaze.
调遣了3辆消防车去救火。

initial
/ i'niʃəl /

adj. 最初的，初始的

The doctor charged $7 for the initial consultation.
医生收出诊费7美元.

同 first
反 final

injection
/ in'dʒekʃən /

n. 注射；注入

The injection of the earth satellite was achieved as planned. 地球卫星按计划被射入轨道。

resourceful
/ ri'sɔːsfəl /

adj. 资源丰富的；足智多谋的

He is the most resourceful and well-supplied cook in the town. 他是全城最有办法，货源又最充裕的厨师。

同 versatile
反 incapable

UNIT 28

fortune
/ 'fɔːtʃən /

n. 财富;运气

He made a fortune by smuggling.
他靠走私发了一笔大财。

---

inquire
/ in'kwaiə /

v. 询问

Please inquire at the next door. 请问隔壁那家。

衍 inquiry *n.*
同 question
搭配 inquire about 打听

---

examine
/ ig'zæmin /

v. 检查

The doctor examined the girl carefully and found her in perfect health.医生为女孩仔细检查身体,发现她健康状况极好。

同 check

---

display
/ di'splei /

vt. 陈列,展览

Shops are displaying summer clothes in their windows.
商店的橱窗里陈列着夏季服装。

同 exhibit

---

as
/ æz /

adv. 同样地

The temperature is as high today as it was yesterday.
今天气温同昨天一样高。

---

fortunate
/ 'fɔːtʃənit /

adj. 幸运的

It was fortunate that no one was killed in the accident.
幸运的是事故中无人丧生。

同 lucky

基础词汇

proceed
/ prəˈsiːd /

vi. 进行，继续下去

The train proceeded at the same speed as before.
列车以原来的速度继续前进。

同 move on
反 stop
搭配 proceed to 进而做

rest
/ rest /

n. 休息；静止

The driver brought the car to a rest.
司机把汽车停了下来。

短语 come to rest 静止下来

treat
/ triːt /

v. 款待

You should treat them with more consideration.
你应该多体谅他们一点。

衍 treatment *n.*

construct
/ kənˈstrʌkt /

vt. 建造

Eyewitness reports construct a detailed description of the man. 目击者的报告构成了有关此人相貌的一幅图像。

衍 construction *n.*

like
/ laik /

v. 希望，愿意

What would you like to do if you have a long vacation?
如果你有个长长的假期，你想做些什么？

probability
/ ˌprɒbəˈbiliti /

n. 可能性

Wars are a serious probability btween the two traditional enemy states in the present state of affairs. 从目前的形式来看，这两个传统上敌对的国家再起战端的可能性非常大。

衍 probable *adj.*
同 possibility
短语 in all probability 十有八九，有可能

基础词汇

拓展词汇

response
/ ri'spɔns /

n. 反应

She made no response.她没有回答。

同 reaction

搭配 in response to 作为对……的反应

responsibility
/ ri͵spɔnsə'biliti /

n. 责任

The driver was cleared of all responsibility for the car accident.司机对这次车祸没有任何责任。

衍 responsible *adj.*

同 duty

反 right

trap
/ træp /

n. 圈套, 陷阱

I knew perfectly well it was a trap .
我完全知道那是圈套。

短语 be caught in a trap 落入陷阱

process
/ prə'ses /

n. 过程

He is quick in his thought processes.
他思维敏捷。

artificial
/ ͵ɑːti'fiʃəl /

adj. 人造的

The ginseng is an artificial plant in South China.
在华南, 人参是人工栽培的植物。

同 man-made

反 natural

status
/ 'steitəs /

n. 地位

Old age has status in the villages .
在农村里年长者受人尊崇。

同 eminence

constitute
/ 'kɔnstitjuːt /

vt. 组成

Twelve months constitute a year.12个月为1年。

exaggerate
/ ig'zædʒəreit /

v. 夸大，夸张

Don't trust what he says easily，for he always exaggerates．不要轻易相信他的话，他总是夸大其词。

衍 exaggeration *n.*

同 overstate

反 understate

die down

平息；变弱

It took a long time for the excitement to die down.
兴奋情绪好久才平息下来。

insistent
/ in'sistənt /

adj. 坚持不懈的

He was insistent on going out.他坚持要出去。

同 persistent

differ from

与……不同

His opinion differs entirely from mine.
他的意见与我的完全不同。

bold
/ bəuld /

adj.& n. 大胆的；粗体

I finally decided on a bold step.
最后，我决定采取一个需要冒险的步骤。

同 daring

反 cowardly

exceed
/ ik'si:d /

v. 超越，胜过；超过其他

His accomplishment exceeded our expectation.
他的成就超过我们原先的期望。

同 surpass

constant
/ 'kɔnstənt /

adj. 不变的；持续的

In history，change is constant. 在历史上变化是不断的。

衍 constancy *n.*

同 permanent

反 changeable

disposal
/ di'spəuzəl /

n. 处理；布置

There is the problem of the safe disposal of radioactive waste.这里存在着安全处理放射性废料的问题。

短语　at one's disposal 由某人支配

steady
/ 'stedi /

adj. 稳固的，稳定的

Her voice was faint but steady.

她的嗓音低微然而深沉。

同 stable

deprive...of

夺去，剥夺

He was deprived of the right to vote.

他被剥夺了选举权。

conspicuous
/ kən'spikjuəs /

adj. 显著的

Her red hat was very conspicuous in the crowd.

她戴的红帽子在人群中非常显眼。

同 noticeable

stationary
/ 'steiʃ(ə)nəri /

a. 固定的；停滞的

The bus remained stationary. 公共汽车停着不开。

同 stagnant

反 moving, shifting

minimize
/ 'minimiaz /

v. 将……减到最少

To minimize the risk of burglary, install a good alarm system.安装可靠的报警设备以减低被盗的风险。

probe
/ prəub /

vt. 探查，查明

Searchlights probed the night sky.探照灯探查夜空。

搭配　probe into 探索，调查

insight
/ 'insait /

n. 洞察力,见识

She has a woman's quick insight into others' characters.
她对人的品格具有女性特有的敏锐眼力。

衍 insightful *adj.*

同 perception

搭配 gain an insight into 深刻了解

dispose
/ di'spəuz /

vt. 处理,处置

All other property which may have come into her possession can be disposed of freely by her. 其他所有可能归到她名下的财产都可以由她自由支配。

衍 disposal *n.*

搭配 dispose of 处理掉

ascend
/ ə'send /

v. 攀登;上升

The airplane ascended into the cloud.
飞机高高飞入云端。

同 rise

反 descend

搭配 ascend to 上升,升高

minimum
/ 'miniməm /

adj. 最小的,最低的

The prices have already been cut to the minimum.
价格已经削减到最低限度。

hoist
/ hɔist /

n.& v. 提升间;升起

The cargo was hoisted on to the ship.货物被吊到了船上。

orientation
/ ˌɔːrien'teiʃən /

n. 方向,方位;定位

The winding trail caused the hikers to lose their orientation.迂回的小路使徒步旅行者们迷失了方向。

steer
/ stiə /

v. 驾驶,掌舵

Have I steered you wrong ?我给你指点错了吗?

短语 steer clear (of) 绕开

UNIT 29

step
/ step /

n. 脚步；步幅
The hospital is only twenty steps away.
医院离此只有20步之遥。
短语 follow in sb.'s steps 效法某人的样子

---

restrict
/ ri'strikt /

vt. 限制，约束
The woods restrict our vision.
被树林一挡，我们的视野变得有限了。
同 restrain

---

dispute
/ di'spjuːt /

v.& n. 争论，辩论
They disputed for hours about where to go.
他们为了去哪里的问题争论了几个小时。
同 argument
反 agreement
短语 beyond dispute 无可置疑的

---

hold
/ həuld /

n.& vt. 持有，拥有
We held each other's hands.我们手握手。
搭配 get hold of 捉住

---

inspection
/ in'spekʃən /

n. 检查，视察
An inspection of the roof showed no leaks.
屋顶经检查未发现有漏洞。
衍 inspect *v.*
同 examination

基础词汇

assault
/ ə'sɔːlt /

n. 攻击，袭击

We made an assault on the enemy fort.
我们向敌人的要塞发动攻击。

同 attack

likely
/ 'laikli /

adj. 可能的

It is likely to rain. 天看来要下雨了。

同 probably

搭配 It is likely that... 有……可能

exceedingly
/ ik'siːdiŋli /

adv. 非常地，极度地

He has done exceedingly well. 他干得很好。

同 extremely

misfortune
/ mis'fɔːtʃən /

n. 不幸，灾祸

He is always ready to help people in misfortune.
他总是乐于帮助遭受厄运的人。

同 disaster

origin
/ 'ɔridʒin /

n. 起源，由来

The reporter traced the story back to its origin.
记者对这报道作了追根究底的调查。

同 root

restore
/ ri'stɔː /

vt. 恢复

He prayed his sight might be restored.
他祈求能够让他恢复视力。

衍 restoration *n.*

consume
/ kən'sjuːm /

v. 消耗,消费

In the mid-seventies, Americans consumed about seventeen million barrels of oil daily. 在70年代中期,美国人每天耗油约达1700万桶。

衍 consumption *n.*

同 exhaust

反 save

stiff
/ stif /

adj. 硬的,僵直的

Her fingers were stiff with cold. 她的手指被冻僵了。

tremble
/ 'trembl /

vi. 颤抖

The room is warm now, but he is still trembling. 房间里现在暖和了,可他仍在哆嗦。

同 shiver

trend
/ trend /

n. 倾向,趋势

The trend of the coastline is to the south. 海岸线是向南延伸的。

同 tendency

virtually
/ 'vəːtʃuəli /

adv. 事实上,实质上

The city virtually disappeared in a tornado. 该城被龙卷风刮得几乎无影无踪。

同 practically

except for

adv. 除……以外

We had a very pleasant time , except for the weather. 除了天公不作美外,我们过得很愉快。

拓展词汇

foster
/ 'fɔstə /

vt.& n. 养育,抚育,培养
She has fostered the child for several months.
他领养这孩子已经几个月了。
同 nourish

disposition
/ dispə'ziʃən /

n. 部署
My car was at his disposition. 我的汽车任他使用。
同 arrangement

consult
/ kən'sʌlt /

v. 商量,商议
Consult your conscience before you act.
在行动之前问一下自己的良心。
衍 consultation *n.*

grip
/ grip /

n. 紧握;掌握
This is the old-fashioned policeman's grip.
这是警察的老式擒拿法。
搭配 come to grips with 与……搏斗

proficient
/ prə'fiʃənt /

adj. 精通的
I'm a reasonably proficient driver.
我开车的技术还算不错。
衍 proficiency *n.*
同 competent

profession
/ prə'feʃən /

n. 职业
He is a carpenter by profession. 他以木工为业。
同 career

拓展词汇

install
/ in'stɔːl /

vt. 安装，安置

My mother installed a refrigerator in the kitchen.
妈妈在厨房内放置了冰箱。

衍 installation *n.*

stick to

粘住；忠于

He was a man who stuck to his friends.
他是一个忠于朋友的人。

dispose of

处置

You may dispose of those books in any way you like.
你可以随意处理掉那些书籍。

productive
/ prə'dʌktiv /

adj. 生产性的；建设性的

The feedback is always more productive than
confrontations.反馈总比对峙更具建设性。

同 constructive

ashamed
/ ə'ʃeimd /

adj. 惭愧的，羞耻的

He was ashamed to confess that he had been in the
wrong.他耻于承认自己不对。

反 proud

搭配 be ashamed of 为……羞愧

提高词汇

boom
/ buːm /

vi. 繁荣

Stock may boom today, but drop tomorrow.
股票可能今天暴涨，但明天又下跌。

同 thrive

反 recede

短语 boom and bust 大繁荣后的不景气

exception
/ ik'sepʃən /

n. 除外，例外

It's been very cold this month, but today is an exception.这个月天气一直很冷,但今天是个意外。

短语　above exception 无可非议

contend
/ kən'tend /

v. 斗争；竞争

She's had a lot of problems to contend with.
她有许多问题要解决。

同 compete

搭配　contend against 搏斗

minority
/ mai'nɔriti /

n. 少数

We are in a pitiful minority. 我们属于可怜巴巴的少数。

forum
/ 'fɔːrəm /

n. 论坛

The letters' page serves as a useful forum for the exchange of readers' views.读者来信版是读者交换意见的有益园地。

bother
/ 'bɔðə /

v. 打扰

That's what bothers me most.
那就是最使我烦恼的一件事情。

同 disturb

搭配　bother one's head about 为……操心

inspire
/ in'spaiə /

v. 激发，启示

The book was inspired by his travels in the Far East.
这本书是他远东旅行的结晶。

衍 inspiration *n.*

201

飞跃词汇

proficiency
/ prə'fiʃənsi /

n. 熟练,精通

Technical proficiency is essential in this job.
这项工作要求很熟练的技术。

衍 proficient *adj.*
同 skillfulness
反 incompetence

ascribe
/ ə'skraib /

vt. 归因于,归咎于

He ascribed his failure to bad luck.
他把自己的失败归咎于运气不好。

同 attribute
搭配 ascribe to 把……归因于

restrain
/ ri'strein /

vt. 抑制,制止

We restrained the boy from jumping. 我们阻止男孩跳跃。

反 encourage

contaminate
/ kən'tæmineit /

v. 污染

Fumes contaminate the air.烟污染空气。

衍 contamination *n.*
同 pollute

stimulate
/ 'stimjuleit /

vt. 刺激;激励

An inspiring teacher can stimulate students to success.
一个鼓励人的老师能够激励学生取得成功。

衍 stimulation *n.*
同 excite
反 depress

UNIT 30

基础词汇

stock
/stɔk/

n. & v. 库存;股票

The fridge was carefully stocked up with food.
冰箱里周到地放满了食品。
短语　out of stock 脱销

foundation
/faun'deiʃən/

n. 基础;基金会

You may be able to get support from an arts foundation.
你可以从文艺基金会得到资助。
同　base

institution
/ˌinsti'tjuːʃən/

n. 习俗;社会公共机构

Giving presents at Christmas is an institution.
圣诞节赠送礼物是一种习俗。

consideration
/kənˌsidə'reiʃən/

n. 体谅;考虑

Cost is a major consideration in buying anything.
买任何东西时价钱是要考虑的主要因素。
同　contemplation
搭配　take ... into consideration 考虑到

profitable
/'prɔfitəbl/

adj. 有利可图的

The advertising campaign proved very profitable.
广告战被证明是非常有利可图的。
衍　profit *n.*
同　lucrative

stove
/stəuv/

n. 炉子

Having a stove in winter is necessary.
在冬天有一个炉子是很有必要的。

limb
/lim/

n. 肢;分支

Please cut off the dead limbs of a tree.
请砍去树上枯死的大枝。

同 branch

miss
/mis/

v. 错过

The house is at the next corner, and you can't miss it.
那房子就在下一个拐角上,你不会找不到。

短语 miss out 错过机会

stream
/striːm/

n. 溪,川

People began coming in streams.
人们开始川流不息地到来。

短语 on stream 投入生产

continual
/kən'tinjuəl/

adj. 连续的,频繁的

There are continual troubles on the frontier, every six months a fighting invariably breaks out.
边界上屡屡出事,每6个月就要打一仗。

同 successive

result
/ri'zʌlt/

n. 结果

The flight was delayed as a result of fog.
因有雾该航班误点。

短语 as a result 结果

disregard
/ˌdisri'gɑːd/

v. 不顾,轻视

He disregarded my advice.
他无视我的忠告。

同 ignore

反 notice

搭配 in disregard of 漠视

基础词汇

excessive
/ik'sesiv/

adj. 过多的

There are excessive rainfalls in the south.
南方的雨水过多。

同 overdone

反 moderate

---

sting
/stiŋ/

v. 刺，刺痛

Pepper stings my tongue.
辣椒辣得我舌头发痛。

---

program
/'prəugræm/

n. 节目

What's on the program?
演出什么节目?

---

popular
/'pɔpjulə/

adj. 通俗的，流行的

Swimming is popular with all ages.
游泳是老老少少都喜爱的。

衍 popularity *n.*

拓展词汇

bounce
/bauns/

v. 弹起

The ball doesn't bounce well.这只球弹性不好。

短语 bounce back 弹回

---

bound
/baund/

n. 界限

There are no bounds to his ambition.
他的野心是无止境的。

搭配 be bound to 注定了的

---

exceptional
/ik'sepʃənəl/

adj. 例外的;异常的

The fireman showed exceptional bravery.
消防队员表现出了非同寻常的勇敢。

同 uncommon

反 average

205

拓展词汇

triumphantly
/trai'ʌmfəntli/

adv. 成功地；耀武扬威地

He showed off his diploma triumphantly.
他得意洋洋地炫耀他的毕业证。

衍 triumph *n.*

hold up

抢劫

Several masked men held up a bank.
几个蒙面人持枪抢劫了银行。

instruct
/in'strʌkt/

vt. 指示

They haven't instructed us where to go.
他们还未指示我们到何处去。

衍 instruction *n.*

contest
/kən'test/

v. 争夺

The birds contested one another for nesting territory.
鸟儿互相争夺筑巢的地盘。

同 compete

mission
/'miʃən/

n. 使命；大使馆

The country maintains over sixty missions abroad.
这个国家在国外设有60多个使馆。

同 task

original
/ə'ridʒənəl/

adj. 最初的，原始的

The land was returned to its original owner.
这块地物归原主了。

同 earliest

反 final

result in

导致

His laziness resulted in his failure.
他的懒惰导致他的失败。

content
/kən'tent/

vt. 满足

We should never content ourselves with book knowledge only. 我们绝不能仅满足于书本知识。

同 satisfy

搭配 be content with 满足

virtue
/'vəːtʃuː/

n. 美德；优点

The school had its drawbacks as well as virtues.
这所学校有其短处，也有其长处。

同 advantage

反 disadvantage

搭配 by virtue of 凭借

assemble
/ə'sembl/

v. 集合

The president assembled the members of Parliament for a special meeting. 总统召及议员举行特别会议。

profound
/prə'faund/

adj. 渊博的，造诣深的

To be a good writer, one needs profound knowledge as well as a vivid imagination. 一个人要想做一名优秀的作家，需要有广博的知识和生动的想象力。

同 deep；intense

反 superficial

fraction
/'frækʃən/

n. 小部分；片断

He purchased the desk and chair at a fraction of its original cost. 他以原价的一部分买下了这张书桌和椅子。

提高词汇

groan
/grəun/

v. 呻吟；抱怨

All kids groaned when I turned off the TV.
我把电视关了，孩子们都抱怨起来。

同 complain

assess
/ə'ses/

vt. 估定，评定

Experts will assess the present state of the economy.
专家将要评价当前的经济状况。

衍 assessment *n.*

instinct
/'instiŋkt/

n. 本能

He is instinct with patriotism.
他充满爱国热情。

同 intuition
短语 by instinct 凭直觉

resume
/ri'zjuːm/

v. 恢复

We'll stop now and resume working at 2 o'clock.
现在我们歇手，两点钟继续工作。

同 continue

trigger
/'trigə/

vt. 引发，引起

The investigation was triggered several months ago.
调查是几个月前开始的。

同 cause

飞跃词汇

dissent
/di'sent/

v. & n. 不同意；异议

The president now faces bitter dissent over his farm policies. 总统现在面临对其农业政策的激烈分歧。

同 disagreement
搭配 dissent from 不同意；持异议

飞
跃
词
汇

premise
/'premis/

n. 前提

I doubt whether the premise is correct.
我倒是质疑这个前提是否正确。

同 hypothesis

assert
/ə'sɜːt/

v. 断言,声称

He asserted his ideas loudly and clearly.
他大声明确地说出自己的想法。

同 claim

dissipate
/'disipeit/

v. 驱散

The wind dissipated the clouds.
风驱散了云。

衍 dissipation *n.*

同 scatter

反 concentrate

UNIT 31

strike
/straik/

n. & vt. 罢工;打击

He struck the dog with his stick .

他用手杖打狗。

短语　on strike 在罢工

continuity
/ˌkɔnti'njuːiti/

n. 连续性,连贯性

Don't break the continuity of the story.

不要打破故事的连续性。

同　progression

distance
/'distəns/

n. 距离

The distance between the store and my house is three miles. 商店与我家之间的距离为3英里。

短语　keep at a distance 保持一定距离

fragile
/'frædʒail/

adj. 易碎的;脆弱的

She looks fragile.

她显得纤弱。

同　brittle

反　strong

fragment
/'frægmənt/

n. & v. 碎片;成为碎片

The vase fell and fragmented into small pieces.

花瓶掉下来,摔成碎片了。

contrary to

与……相反

The decision was contrary to my wishes.

决议与我的愿望相反。

基础词汇

stretch
/stretʃ/

v. 伸展,伸长

She was stretched on the bed .

她舒展着身子躺在床上。

短语 at a stretch 不停地,一口气地

associate
/ə'səuʃieit/

v. (使)发生联系

They were closely associated with each other during the war.在战争期间,他们的关系很密切。

衍 association *n.*

搭配 associate with 把……联系在一起

holy
/'həuli/

adj. 神圣的,圣洁的

A mother's holy love for her child is crucial for his (her) healthy development.母亲对孩子圣洁的爱对于他(她)们的健康成长至关重要。

同 sacred

mobile
/'məubail/

adj. 可移动的

The population of this city has always been mobile.

这个城市的人口一直在流动。

衍 mobility *n.*

同 movable

反 stationary

exclude
/ik'sklu:d/

vt. 把……排除在外

That price excludes accommodation.

那价钱不包括住宿。

反 include

prohibit
/prə'hibit/

vt. 禁止,阻止

Nuclear powers are prohibited from selling this technology. 禁止核大国出售该项技术。

衍 prohibition *n.*

同 ban

反 permit

搭配 prohibit from 禁止

基础词汇

limitation
/ˌlimiˈteiʃən/

n. 限制,局限性

It would exceed the limitation of this report if discussed adequately.如果充分讨论它,就会超越了这个报告的范围。

衍 limit *v.*

stress
/stres/

n. 压力;强调

Not all of us can cope with the stresses of modern life. 我们中并非所有的人都能应付现代生活的紧张压力。

同 pressure

promising
/ˈprɔmisiŋ/

adj. 有希望的,有前途的

The weather is promising.
天气可望好转。

insure
/inˈʃuə/

v. 给……上保险

He insured his house against fire.
他给自己的房屋保了火险。

衍 insurance *n.*

拓展词汇

asset
/ˈæset/

n. 资产

He has invested five percent of his assets in gold.
他把自己5%的资产投资于黄金。

draw back

退却,缩回

The dog didn't draw back at the sight of the strangers.
这狗看到这些陌生人并不后退。

exclaim
/ikˈskleim/

vi. 呼喊,惊叫

He exclaimed that he was hungry.
他叫喊说他饿了。

衍 exclamation *n.*

搭配 exclaim at 大声叫喊

originality
/əˌridʒi'næliti/

n. 独创性；新颖；起初

Lawyers emerged from originality in the 18th century and became key members of the commercial colonies.

律师从18世纪开始出现，并成为商业殖民地的主要成员。

prominent
/'prɔminənt/

adj. 卓越的；显著的

His nose is too prominent.

他的鼻子太高了。

衍 prominence *n.*

同 eminent

反 inconspicuous

distill
/di'stil/

v. 蒸馏；提取

His important writings are distilled into one volume.

他的重要著作已精选汇编成一卷子。

insult
/in'sʌlt/

vt. 侮辱，凌辱

She insulted him by calling him a coward.

她辱骂他是个胆小鬼。

同 abuse

反 compliment

短语　add insult to injury 雪上加霜

strengthen
/'streŋθən/

v. 加强，巩固

Your words strengthened my heart .

您的话增强了我的决心。

同 consolidate

反 weaken

assimilate
/ə'simileit/

v. 同化

He was assimilated to the village way of life.

他被乡村的生活方式所同化。

衍 assimilation *n.*

搭配　assimilate into 使同化

拓展词汇

contract
/kən'trækt/

n. & v. 合同，契约
The farmer contracted to lease his land.
那农场主立约出租土地。

---

execute
/'eksikjuːt/

vt. 执行；处死
Your order will be executed as soon as possible.
你的命令将尽快被执行。

衍 execution *n.*
同 implement

---

drive at

意指，用意
What on earth are you driving at? Can't you come to the point? 你究竟要说什么？你不能直截了当些吗？

提高词汇

grope
/grəup/

v. 摸索
She groped for her glasses in the bag.
她在包里摸眼镜。

同 fumble
搭配 grope for 在暗处摸索

---

mob
/mɔb/

n. 乌合之众
He pushed his way through the mob.
他从人群中挤过去。

---

contradiction
/ˌkɔntrə'dikʃən/

n. 反驳，矛盾
The chairman wouldn't listen to any contradiction of his opinions.
主席不愿意倾听任何反对意见。

衍 contradict *v.*

---

originate
/ə'ridʒineit/

v. 起源；发生
Her book originated from a short story.
她的书从一篇短篇小说发展而成。

搭配 originate from 发源，来自

提高词汇

prolong
/prə'lɔŋ/

vt. 延长，拖延

He enjoyed the situation and wanted to prolong it.
他对处境很满意，希望长此不变。

同 lengthen
反 shorten

retreat
/ri'triːt/

vi. & *n.* 撤退，退却

The troops were starved to retreat.
士兵们饿得只好撤退。

同 withdraw
反 advance
短语　beat a retreat 打退堂鼓

Week⑤Day③

assign
/ə'sain/

vt. 分配，指派

They assigned me a small room.
他们分给我一个小房间。

distinction
/di'stiŋkʃən/

n. 区别，差别

His novels tend to blur the distinctions between reality and fantasy.他的小说往往模糊了现实和幻想的区别。

同 difference
反 resemblance
搭配　make a distinction 区分，辨别

飞跃词汇

boycott
/'bɔikɔt/

vt. 联合抵制

Supermarkets boycott uncooperated manufacturers.
超市抵制不合作的制造商。

bracket
/'brækit/

n. & *v.* 括弧；归类

The problems were bracketed into groups.
问题被分门别类做了归纳。

retrieve
/ri'tri:v/

v. 重新得到；找回

Some dogs can be trained to retrieve games.

有些狗可被训练来衔回猎物。

衍 retrieval *n.*

同 restore

trivial
/'triviəl/

adj. 琐细的，微不足道的

Frankly speaking, your article is very good except for some trivial mistakes in grammar. 坦率地说，除了一些微不足道的语法错误外，你的文章很不错。

UNIT 32

break
/breik/

n. & v. 休息；破裂

I broke a leg when skiing.
我在滑雪时摔断了一条腿。

exhaust
/ig'zɔːst/

v. & n. 用尽；废气

Some scientists are concerned about long-term expo-sure to car exhaust fumes. 一些科学家对人们长期接触汽车废气感到担心。

衍 exhaustion *n.*

breakthrough
/'breikθruː/

n. 突破

It demonstrates a major technological breakthrough.
这标志着一次重要的技术突破。

contribute
/kən'tribjuːt/

v. 贡献

She never contributes to the discussion.
她在讨论中从不发表意见。

衍 contribution *n.*

搭配 contribute to 做贡献

distinguish
/di'stiŋgwiʃ/

v. 区别,辨别

I can distinguish them by their uniforms.
我能根据他们穿的制服辨认他们。

同 tell apart

短语 distinguish oneself 使杰出,使著名

convenience
/kən'viːniəns/

n. 便利，方便

In the past, most royal marriages were marriages of convenience, arranged for political reasons. 过去大部分的皇室婚姻都是利益婚姻，是基于政治原因的婚姻。

短语　at your convenience 在你方便的时候

mock
/mɔk/

v. 嘲笑

He had mocked her modest ambitions.
他曾嘲笑她那一副小家子气的种种抱负。

同 ridicule
搭配　mock sb./sth. 嘲笑

distorted
/di'stɔːtid/

adj. 扭歪的，受到曲解的

The newspaper gave a distorted account of the accident.
报纸对那起事故作了歪曲的报道。

衍 distortion *n.*

convention
/kən'venʃən/

n. 习俗，惯例；大会

Using the right hand to shake hands is a convention.
握手时用右手是一种习惯。

衍 conventional *adj.*
同 custom

promotion
/prə'məuʃən/

n. 提拔；促进

I want a job with good prospects for promotion.
我想找一份有很好晋升前景的工作。

衍 promote *vt.*

struggle
/'strʌgl/

n. & v. 竞争；努力

We will not surrender without a struggle.
我们绝不会不战而降。

frank
/fræŋk/

adj. **坦白的,率直的**

To be frank, he is not qualified for the job.
坦率地说,他不能胜任这份工作。

同 candid

反 restrained

短语　to be frank 坦率地说

revenue
/'revinju:/

n. **收入;税收**

The editor was concerned for the drop in advertsing revenue.编辑对于广告费收入的减少极为关注。

distribute
/di'stribju(:)t/

v. **分发;分配**

The teacher distributes students into 4 groups.
老师把学生分成了4组。

衍 distribution *n.*

搭配　distribute...to 分配

prompt
/prɔmpt/

adj. **敏捷的,迅速的**

She was very prompt in answering my letter.
她给我写回信非常及时。

assume
/ə'sju:m/

vt. **假定,设想**

She must be assumed to be innocent until proven guilty.
再被证实有罪之前,应该拟订她是无辜的。

同 suppose

integrity
/in'tegriti/

n. **正直;完整**

The territorial and sovereign integrity of our nation depends on working together. 我们国家领土和主权的完整要靠大家齐心协力。

同 completeness

反 fragmentation

assurance
/əˈʃuərəns/

n. 确信；保证

He gave an assurance that the work would be completed by Friday.他保证能在星期五之前完成这项工作。

衍 assure *vt.*

同 promise

at ease

安逸，自由自在

His legs were weary, but his mind was at ease.
他的双腿很疲乏，但心情舒畅。

framework
/ˈfreimwəːk/

n. 框架，结构

All the cases can be considered within the framework of the existing rules.一切情况都可依据现行的规章加以考虑。

gross
/grəus/

adj. & n. 总的；总额

The gross for the year is $50,000.
年总收入5万美金。

同 whole

短语 in the gross 大体上，总的说来

drop out

退出；放弃

Teenagers who drop out of high school have trouble finding jobs.高中未念完而辍学的年轻人不容易找工作。

controversy
/ˈkɔntrəvəːsi/

n. 辩论

They spark a controversy over human rights.
他们在人权问题上引起一场大辩论。

衍 controversial *adj.*

同 disagreement

ornament
/'ɔːnəmənt/

n. 装饰

A scarf can be a good ornament to one's clothing.
围巾可以很好地衬托服装。

同 decorate

proof
/pruːf/

n. 证据

Can you give proof that you are Spanish?
你能提出证据证明你是西班牙人吗?

衍 prove *vt.*

troop
/truːp/

n. 军队;(人或动物的)一群

Troops of deer are running.
成群的鹿在奔跑。

at intervals

不时地

The monotonous noise would stop at intervals, then resume after a while.那单调的噪音时而停一会儿,然后又响起。

exempt
/ig'zempt/

v. 免除

Nobody should be exempted from an examination.
没人可以免考。

搭配 exempt from 豁免

exert
/ig'zəːt/

v. 施加(压力等)

He's been exerting a lot of pressure on me to change my mind.他一直在施加种种压力让我改变主意。

短语 exert oneself 努力,尽力

integrate
/'intigreit/

v. 使成整体

The different ideas have been integrated into one u-niform plan. 不同的意见全部融入了一个统一的计划。

衍 integration *n.*

同 unify

搭配 integrate ... into 使合并

prone
/prəun/

adj. 倾向于

People are more prone to make mistakes when they are tired. 人们疲劳时更容易出差错。

搭配 prone to 有……倾向的

intellectual
/ˌinti'lektʃuəl/

adj. & n. 智力的;知识分子

Teaching is an intellectual occupation.
教书是一种用脑力的职业。

moderate
/'mɔdəreit/

vt. 适中;温和

The weather was beginning to moderate.
天气开始变得气温适中。

衍 moderation *n.*

短语 in moderate 适度地,有节制地

revenge
/ri'vendʒ/

n. & vt. 报仇

Hamlet wanted revenge his father's murder.
哈姆雷特要报杀父之仇。

衍 retribution *n.*

搭配 take revenge on 向某人报复

stroke
/strəuk/

n. 一次努力;打击

Your idea was a stroke of genius.
你的主意真了不起。

短语 at a stroke 一下子,一举

orthodox
/'ɔːθədɒks/

adj. **正统的;传统的**

Her ideas are very orthodox.
她的思想非常合乎规范。

stumble
/'stʌmbl/

vi. **绊倒**

He stumbled on a stone.
他在石头上绊了一跤。

同 stagger

linger
/'lɪŋgə/

vi. **逗留**

She lingered for a moment at the door.
她在门口逗留了一会儿。

同 hang around

短语 linger on 流连,留恋

intact
/ɪn'tækt/

adj. **完整无缺的**

To the waiter's relief, the plates were left intact after being dropped on the floor. 令服务生欣慰的是，盘子掉到地板上后完好无损。

同 complete

UNIT 33

intense
/in'tens/

adj. 强烈的,剧烈的

The army and the police remained under intense pressure in the Korean peninsula. 朝鲜半岛的军队和警察一直都处于高压之下。

同 severe

convey
/kən'vei/

vt. 传达;运送

A chimney conveys smoke to the outside.
烟囱将烟排送到室外。

同 carry

expand
/ik'spænd/

vt. 扩张

She expanded her article into a book.
她把自己的文章扩写成一本书。

衍 expansion *n.*

同 extend

revolt
/ri'vəult/

n. & v. 反叛;起义

The peasants' revolt was gaining momentum.
农民起义的声势越来越大。

attack
/ə'tæk/

n. & v. 进攻,攻击

The watchdog attacked the intruder.
看门狗扑向闯入的人。

同 assault

反 defend

短语 launch an attack against 攻击

frequently
/'fri:kwəntli/

adv. 频繁地

Bricks are frequently used as building materials.
砖头经常被用来作建筑材料。

同 often

ground
/graund/

n. 范围

They managed to cover quite a lot of ground in a short program. 他们设法在一个短小的节目中包罗多方面的内容。

短语　on the ground 当场，在现场

style
/stail/

n. 风格

What style of furniture do you like?
你喜欢什么式样的家具?

intensive
/in'tensiv/

adj. 精深的；透彻的

They teach you English in an intensive course lasting just a week. 他们用一周时间教速成英语课程。

other
/'ʌðə/

adj. 其他的，另外的

Now open your other eye.
好了，睁开你另一只眼吧。

link
/liŋk/

n. & v. 联系

Their names have been linked together in newspaper reports. 在报纸的报道中，他们的名字已经被联系在一起。

短语　link up 连接起来，联系在一起

properly
/'prɔpəli/

adv. 适当地

She will have to learn how to behave properly.
她要懂得检点些。

disturbed
/di'stə:bt/

adj. 困扰的

He was disturbed at recalling the sight.
回想起那情景，他忐忑不安。

property
/'prɔpəti/

n. 财产

The hotel is not responsible for any loss or damage to guests' personal property. 房客个人财产的丢失或损坏宾馆概不负责。

reward
/ri'wɔ:d/

n. & vt. 报酬，酬劳

The rewards of art are not to be measured in money.
艺术的报偿是不能以金钱来衡量的。

tunnel
/'tʌnl/

n. 隧道，地道

The tunnel sloped downward, and when Ronald emerged from it he halted. 地道向下倾斜，当罗纳德从地道出来时，他一下停住了。

at large

逍遥自在地；详细地

The question is discussed at large in my report.
我在报告中对该问题做了详细的探讨。

breed
/bri:d/

v. (使)繁殖；抚养

Some animals will not breed when kept in cages.
有些动物关在笼内就不产崽。

at stake

危险

His own personal future was at stake.
他个人的前途很成问题。

convince
/kən'vins/

vt. 使确信，使信服

Powerful advertising can convince people to buy almost everything. 攻势强大的广告几乎能使人们乐意买下任何东西。

同 persuade

搭配 be convinced of 使……信服

distraction
/di'strækʃən/

n. 注意力分散

There are too many distractions here to work properly. 这儿分心的事太多，让人无法正常工作。

同 diversion

subject to

使服从，使遭受

Astronauts are subjected to all kinds of tests before they are actually sent up in a spacecraft. 宇航员被送往宇宙飞船之前都要接受各种各样的测试。

fraud
/frɔːd/

n. 欺骗

His explanation was a fraud. 他的解释是骗人的鬼话。

同 deception

literacy
/'litərəsi/

n. 有文化；有读写能力

There is the lowering of the level of literacy. 文化水准有所下降。

convert
/kən'vəːt/

v. 使转变

He was converted to the Darwinian theory. 他转而信仰达尔文的进化论。

同 transform

搭配 convert into 使转变

other than　　不同于；除了

The truth is quite other than what you think.
事实的真相和你想的完全不一样。

intelligence
/in'telidʒəns/

n. 智力；聪明

She thinks that his decision to study abroad is a decision of intelligence. 她认为他决定出国留学是明智的。

衍 intelligent *adj.*

---

converge
/kən'və:dʒ/

v. 聚合

The roads converged at the stadium.
各条道路在体育场汇聚。

同 intersect

反 separate

---

hop
/hɔp/

v. 单脚跳

Several frogs were hopping about on the lawn.
有几只青蛙在草地上跳来跳去。

同 jump

---

modification
/ˌmɔdifi'keiʃn/

n. 更改

This led to the modification of traditional wedding customs. 这导致了对传统婚礼习俗的修改。

衍 modify *v.*

---

monetary
/'mʌnitəri/

adj. 货币的，金钱的

The prices of all goods are expressed in terms of a common monetary unit. 所有的商品价格都用通用货币单位表示。

同 financial

exhibit
/ig'zibit/

vt. 展出；展示

The teacher exhibits a very good attitude towards his students. 老师对学生表现出很好的态度。

衍 exhibition *n.*

同 show

diverse
/dai'vəːs/

adj. 不同的；多种多样的

My sister and I have diverse ideas on how to raise children.在怎样养育孩子的问题上，我姐姐与我有迥然不同的看法。

衍 diversity *n.*

exile
/'eksail/

n. & vt. 放逐，流放

After an exile of ten years, her uncle returned to Britain. 她叔叔背井离乡十年后返回英国。

stun
/stʌn/

vt. 使惊吓

I was stunned by the news of his death.
我得知他的死讯非常震惊。

同 shock

propel
/prə'pel/

vt. 推进；驱使

They propelled him into the room.
他们把他推入房间。

同 impel

subordinate
/sə'bɔːdinit/

adj. & n. & v. 从属的；下属；从属

She is subordinate to her husband in every way.
她在任何方面都顺从丈夫。

同 inferior

反 superior

飞跃词汇

propaganda
/ˌprɔpə'gændə/

n. 宣传

That's mere propaganda.

那不过是宣传而已。

同 promulgation

---

brew
/bruː/

v. 酝酿

The children are brewing a pleasant surprise for their father's birthday. 孩子们在暗中筹划，准备在父亲的生日那天送他一件意想不到的好礼物。

同 devise

---

reverse
/ri'vəːs/

n. & adj. 相反；相反的

The truth is just the reverse.

真实情况恰好相反。

衍 reversal *n.*

短语 reverse oneself (on sth.)承诺错误；放弃(立场)

UNIT 34

brief
/briːf/

adj. 短暂的
My acquaintance with him is brief.
我与他相识的全过程时间不长。
同 short-lived
搭配 make brief of 使简短

subsequent
/'sʌbsikwənt/

adj. 后来的
Most countries in Europe were in a mess during the period subsequent to World War Ⅱ. 二战后的一段时期中,大部分欧洲国家陷入了窘境。

expenditure
/ik'spenditʃə/

n. 支出,花费
Government expenditure on education is rising.
政府在教育上的开支正在增加。
同 expense

attempt
/ə'tempt/

n. & vt. 努力;尝试
He was guilty of attempted robbery.
他犯抢劫未遂罪。
同 endeavor
短语 in an attempt to 试图做……

frontier
/'frʌntiə/

n. 边境
There are frequent frontier disputes.
总有边境冲突。
同 boundary

基础词汇

interfere
/ˌintəˈfiə/

vi. 干预,打扰

Dose the vacuum cleaner interfere with radio or TV?
真空吸尘器干扰收音机和电视吗?
搭配　interfere in(with)干涉

---

do
/duː/

vt. 做;实行

Do what I tell you.
按照我说的去做。

---

monitor
/ˈmɔnitə/

vt. 监控

You'll have to monitor your eating constantly.
你一定要经常注意控制饮食。

同 supervise

---

ridiculous
/riˈdikjuləs/

adj. 荒谬的,可笑的

What a ridiculous idea!
多荒唐的主意!

---

intent
/inˈtent/

n. 意图

The man was charged with intent to murder.
那人被指控蓄意谋杀。

同 intention
搭配　be intent on 专注于

---

end up

结束,告终

How does the story end up?
故事的结局如何?

---

face up to

(勇敢地)面对,正视

The explorers faced up to terrible hardships with constant cheerfulness. 探险家们一直以愉快的心情面对极大的艰险。

attain
/ə'tein/

v. 达到，获得

He has attained the age of ninety.
他已达90高龄。

衍 attainment *n.*

同 accomplish

cope with

与……竞争；应付

There are more work than I could cope with.
工作多得我应付不过来。

do away with

废除

They did away with uniforms at that shool years ago.
那个学校在多年前就取消了校服。

intention
/in'tenʃən/

n. 意图，目的

My intention is to stay.
我愿意留下来。

衍 intentional *adj.*

同 purpose

live up to

实践，做到

You should live up to your promise.
你应当遵守诺言。

propose
/prə'pəuz/

v. 计划；建议；求婚

I propose an early start tomorrow.
我打算明天早早出发。

同 plan

短语 propose（marriage）to 向某人求婚

otherwise
/'ʌðəwaiz/

adv. & adj. 另外；否则

He reminded me of what I should otherwise have forgotten.他提醒了我那件不然我可能会忘记的事。

out of question 毫无疑问

She knew that a holiday this year was out of question.
她知道今年肯定有假期。

costly
/'kɔstli/

adj. 昂贵的;贵重的

Some of the standards are costly to shipowners.
要达到有些标准对船主来说代价很高。

同 expensive
反 cheap

mood
/muːd/

n. 心情,情绪

Mary is in a good mood this morning.
玛丽今天早上心情不错。

短语 be in the mood to do sth. 有心思做某事

proportion
/prə'pɔːʃən/

n. 比例

Clearly, the amount of money people save increases in reverse proportion to the amount they spend. 显然,人们的储蓄额与他们的开销成反比增长。

搭配 in proportion to 与……成比例

rewarding
/ri'wɔːdiŋ/

adj. 有益的;值得的

Reading can be very rewarding for everyone.
阅读对人人都会有莫大的好处。

同 worthwhile

correspond to 相一致;相符合

His expenses do not correspond to his income.
他的支出与收入不相称。

horizon
/hə'raizn/

n. 地平线;(知识,思想等的)范围

The sun has sunk below the horizon.
太阳已沉落在地平线下。

expel
/ik'spel/

v. 驱逐；开除

The student was expelled for cheating.
这个学生因作弊而被开除。

同 oust

substitute
/'sʌbstitjuːt/

n. & v. 替代品；代替

We must substitute a new chair for the broken one.
我们这把破损的椅子得换把新的。

同 alternate

短语 substitute for 用……代替

attend to

专心；照顾

He should attend better to his studies.
他应该更专心于学习。

subtle
/'sʌtl/

adj. 微妙的

His whole attitude has undergone a subtle change.
他的整个态度已经有了微妙的变化。

同 subtlety *n.*

expedition
/ˌekspi'diʃən/

n. 远征；探险

We did an expedition to Burnham Beaches.
我们到伯纳姆山毛榉林去考察了一次。

divert
/dai'vəːt/

v. 转移，转向，使高兴

Traffic is being diverted from the main road because of the accident. 由于事故，车辆行人绕道而行。

同 distract

搭配 divert from 转移……注意力

bribe
/braib/

n. & vt. 贿赂

He had been bribed into silence. 他被收买而闭口不言。

235

飞跃词汇

counsel
/'kaunsəl/

vt. 劝告，忠告

She counseled them not to accept this agreement.
她劝告他们不要接受这个协议。

同 advise

prospect
/'prɔspekt/

n. 前景，前途

Is there any prospect of success?能指望成功吗?

同 outlook

rigorous
/'rigərəs/

adj. 严格的;严厉的

Students must finish rigorous programs of studying to become a doctor. 学生必须完成严格的学习任务才能成为医生。

同 strict

反 undemanding

fringe
/frindʒ/

n. 边缘;刘海

She has a fringe and glasses.她额前有刘海儿,戴着眼镜。

同 edge

grudge
/grʌdʒ/

vt. 恶意;怨恨

I always feel she has a grudge against me, although I don't know what wrong I've done her.我总觉得她在恨我,但我并不知道自己有什么地方亏待了她。

同 spite

litter
/'litə/

n. & vt. 垃圾;乱丢

The children picked up all the litter on the playground.
孩子们把乱扔在操场上的废纸等杂物都拾了起来。

同 clutter

substantial
/səb'stænʃl/

adj. 数目大的;可观的

We had a substantial wheat crop this year.
我们今年小麦丰收。

同 considerable

反 tiny

UNIT 35

attendant
/ə'tendənt/

n. 服务员；陪侍

She served as an attendant on the bride at a wedding.
她是婚礼上的伴娘。

---

bring
/briŋ/

v. 带来；产生

Will you bring her to Tom's party?
请你带她去汤姆的宴会，好不好？

搭配　bring about 导致，引起

---

protection
/prə'tekʃən/

n. 保护

Such a thin coat gives little protection against the cold.
这样单薄的上衣不能御寒。

衍　protect *vt.*

---

outrage
/'autreidʒ/

n. 暴行

Setting the house on fire was an outrage.
纵火烧房子是一种暴行。

同　atrocity

---

attentive
/ə'tentiv/

adj. 注意的；专心的

He is attentive to what he is doing.
他对他手头的工作很专心。

同　mindful

反　apathetic

短语　be attentive to 注意的，专心的

---

domestic
/də'mestik/

adj. 家庭的；国内的

His second marriage has made him very domestic.
他的第二次婚姻使他变得非常喜欢家庭生活了。

expense
/ik'spens/

n. 费用

All of her expenses are being paid by her company.
她的一切开支都由她的公司支付。

同 expenditure

短语 at（one's）expense 由某人付费

guarantee
/ˌgærən'ti/

n. & vt. 保证

This product is guaranteed against faulty workmanship for 90 days after purchase. 本产品自购买之日起90天保证工艺没有缺陷。

intermediate
/ˌintə'miːdiət/

adj. 中级的

This course is of intermediate difficulties.
这个课程难度中等。

experimental
/ikˌspəri'mentl/

adj. 实验的

It is still in an experimental stage.
这仍处于试验阶段。

rise
/raiz/

v. 上升；起身

He rose immediately to reply.
他立即起立回答。

loan
/ləun/

n. & v. 贷款；借

May I have a loan of your dictionary?
我可以借用一下你的词典吗?

短语 on loan 暂借的

locate
/ləu'keit/

v. 位于

His house is located on the edge of the city.
他的房屋坐落在市区的边缘。

衍 location *n.*

such
/sʌtʃ/

adj. 这样的

I have never seen such a sight.
我从未见过这种景象。

短语　such as to 到如此程度以致

cover
/'kʌvə/

v. 盖住；包含

Snow covered the highway.
大雪覆盖了公路。

短语　cover up 掩盖，掩饰

protest
/prə'test/

n. & v. 抗议

The minister was greeted with a chorus of protest.
这位部长迎来了一片抗议之声。

搭配　make a protest against 对某事提出抗议
　　　without protest 心甘情愿的

morality
/mə'ræləti/

n. 道德；道义

We talked about the morality of fox-hunting.
我们谈论猎狐的道义性。

同　rightness

counterpart
/'kauntəpɑ:t/

n. 极相似的人或物

The British Queen is the counterpart of the German president. 英国女王相当于德国的总统。

interior
/in'tiəriə/

adj. 内部的，内在的

This passage has interior meaning.
这一段文章隐有深意。

反　exterior

frown
/fraun/

vi. 皱眉

His face frowned.
他面有愠色。

短语　give sb. a frown of disapproval
　　　向某人做出不赞成的表情

attraction
/ə'trækʃən/

n. 吸引力

A zoo has great attraction for children.
动物园对小孩具有很大的吸引力。

衍 attract *vt.*

bring about

使发生,致使

This policy brings about many improvements in the employment of women. 这个政策在雇佣妇女方面带来许多改进。

outline
/'autlain/

n. 大纲;略图

We agreed on an outline of the proposal.
我们对此建议的一个提纲达成一致意见。

interpretation
/inˌtə:pri'teiʃən/

n. 解释;口译

People often give different interpretations of the past.
人们往往对过去作出不同的解释。

衍 interpret *v.*

同 rendition

ripe
/'raip/

adj. 成熟的

The kitchen garden is ripe with tomatoes.
菜园里的番茄已长熟了。

同 mature

反 untimely

短语 Soon ripe, soon rotten. 早慧早衰

count
/kaunt/

v. 数,计算

There will be ten guests, not counting the children.
孩子不算,将有10个客人。

同 calculate

搭配 count on 依靠

240

拓展词汇

rival
/ˈraivəl/

n. & v. 竞争者,对手;对抗

There was no rival to him as a poet.
作为诗人,无人可与他媲美。

同 opponent

反 partner

辨析 rival 竞争,匹敌

compete 比赛,比胜

contend 竞争,奋斗,强调努力和决心

suicide
/ˈsjuːisaid/

n. 自杀

There is a connection between a rising rate of unemployment and a rising suicide rate. 在日趋上升的失业率和日趋上升的自杀率之间有着某种联系。

短语 commit a suicide 自杀

提高词汇

hospitality
/ˌhɔspiˈtæliti/

n. 好客

The natives are noted for their hospitality.
当地人以好客著称。

衍 hospitable *adj.*

coward
/ˈkauəd/

n. 懦弱的人,胆小的人

John was coward enough to agree.
约翰真是个胆小鬼,居然会同意。

短语 Cowards are cruel. 懦夫必残忍。

frugal
/ˈfruːgəl/

adj. 节俭的

She is a frugal house wife.
她是个俭省的主妇。

同 thrifty

mortal
/ˈmɔːtl/

n. & adj. 凡人;必死的

Remember that man is mortal.
人总有一死。

241

提高词汇

suck
/sʌk/

v. 吸,吮

Can beer be sucked through a straw?
啤酒能用麦管吸着喝吗?
短语 suck in 吸收

succession
/sək'seʃən/

n. 连续;继承

His succession as headmaster was not in any doubt.
他接任校长是毫无疑问的。
短语 in succession 连续的

sufficient
/sə'fiʃənt/

adj. 充分的,足够的

A word to the wise is sufficient.
有灵犀者一点就通。
衍 sufficiency *n.*
同 adequate
反 scarce

prototype
/'prəutətaip/

n. 原型

This is a prototype airplane produced by our company.
这就是我们公司生产的样机。

飞跃词汇

doctrine
/'dɔktrin/

n. 教条

It was one of my father's doctrines that pain was good for people.   我父亲的信条之一是痛苦对人有好处。
同 tenet

dodge
/dɔdʒ/

v. 避开,躲避

He dodged cleverly when I threw the ball at him.
我将球掷向他时,他机敏地躲开了。
同 avoid
反 encounter

242

飞跃词汇

prospective
/prə'spektiv/

adj. 预期的

He is unhappy about the prospective loss.
他对可能出现的损失感到不快。

同 anticipated

expire
/ik'spaiə/

v. 期满；终止

His term of office expires this year.
他的任期到今年届满。

同 cease

UNIT 36

romantic
/rəu'mæntik/

adj. 传奇式的;浪漫的

She is as romantic as a child of sixteen.

她像16岁的孩子那样爱浪漫。

衍 romance *n.*

---

crash
/kræʃ/

n. 碰撞;破裂(声)

The vase fell on the floor with a crash.

花瓶哗啦一声掉在地上。

同 smash

frustrate
/frʌ'streit/

v. 挫败

After two hours' frustrating delay, our train at last arrived. 经过两个小时令人沮丧的耽搁后, 我们的火车终于到达了。

衍 frustration *n.*

同 thwart

fulfil
/ful'fil/

vt. 履行;符合

Does your job fulfil your expectation?

你的工作符合你的预想吗?

衍 fulfilment *n.*

短语 fulfil oneself 完全实现自己的抱负

---

guard
/gɑːd/

n. & vi. 守卫

The dog guarded the child day and night.

狗日夜守护着那个孩子。

短语 on guard 警惕, 提防

基础词汇

sum up

概括

My mood could be summed up by the single word "boredom". 我的心情可以用"厌倦"这一个词来概括。

host
/həust/

n. 主人

I was away so my son acted as host.
我那时不在家,所以由我的儿子招待客人。

doubt
/daut/

v. 怀疑

I don't doubt that he will come on time.
我肯定他会准时来的。

同 suspect

短语 no doubt 无疑的,确实的

interrupt
/ˌintə'rʌpt/

v. 打断;插嘴

Traffic was interrupted by a snowstorm.
交通被暴风雪阻断。

衍 interruption *n.*

outside
/'autsaid/

n. & adv. & prep. 外面

He opened the door from the outside.
他从外面开门。

短语 outside broadcast 实况广播

void
/vɔid/

adj. 空的

She is void of facial expressions.
她的面部没有任何表情。

搭配 be void of 没有,缺乏

outwardly
/'autwədli/

adv. 表面地,外观上地

Outwardly, she looked calm.
从表面看来她很冷静。

roar
/rɔː/

v. 喧嚣

The streets roar.
街上一片喧嚣。

---

suit
/sjuːt/

v. 适合

This house suits our requirements.
这所房子符合我们的要求。

---

draft
/drɑːft/

n. 草稿

He's now revising the first draft of his essay.
他正在修改他那篇文章的初稿。

短语　on draft（啤酒）散装的

---

violence
/'vaiələns/

n. 猛烈；暴力

He flung open the door with unnecessary violence .
他过分用劲地猛然把门打开。

衍　violent *adj.*

attribute
/ə'tribju(ː)t/

n. & v. 属性，品质；归结于

He attributed his success to hard work.
他把他的成功归因于艰苦努力。

同　ascribe

搭配　attribute sth. to 把……归结于

---

brisk
/brisk/

adj. 活泼的

The food is so-so, but the service is brisk.
饭菜不怎么样，但上菜上得很快。

同　lively

反　torpid

短语　brisk up 使轻快，使活跃

dominate
/'dɔmineit/

v. 支配

She dominated the meeting by sheer force of character.
她单凭个人气势就镇住了会场。

衍 domination *n.*

同 control

explicit
/ik'splisit/

adj. 清楚的

He has an explicit understanding of the problem.
她对这个问题有清晰的认识。

同 clear

反 ambiguous

crack down on
制裁；镇压

Police take measures to crack down on crimes.
警方采取行动制裁犯罪行为。

craze
/kreiz/

n. 狂热

The actor is quite the craze.
这位演员正红极一时。

同 vogue

interval
/'intəvəl/

n. 时间间隔

He returned to work after an interval in hospital.
他住院一段时间以后又回来上班了。

搭配 at intervals 间隔

summon up
鼓起(勇气)；振作(精神)

She tried to summon up the memory of the event.
她试图回想起那件往事。

look into
窥视；观察；调查

I saw Mary looking into a shop window.
我看见玛丽正朝商店橱窗里观看。

exploit
/ik'splɔit/

v. 开发;剥削

Their talents might be exploited to the full.
他们的才能可能得到充分的利用。

衍 exploitation *n.*
同 utilize

turn down

拒绝

I was turned down for the job.
我想做这工作但被拒绝。

authorize
/'ɔːθəraiz/

vt. 批准

The dictionary authorizes two spellings for this word.
词典认为这个词可有两种拼法。

同 permit

explore
/ik'splɔː/

vt. 探险,探测,探究

Businessmen explore the surroundings of the capital.
商人们考察首都的环境。

衍 exploration *n.*
同 probe

superficial
/ˌsjuːpə'fiʃəl/

adj. 表面的,肤浅的

I have only a superficial knowledge of this subject.
我对这个问题仅略知皮毛。

同 shallow
反 profound

brittle
/'britl/

adj. 易碎的;尖利的

She has a brittle tone of voice.
她的声调尖利。

同 crisp

lodger
/'lɔdʒə/

n. 寄宿者,投宿者

Lodgers live in that hotel.
房客住在那家旅馆。

提高词汇

authentic
/ɔː'θentik/

adj. 可信的；货真价实的
Is that an authentic Roman statue, or a morden copy?
这是罗马雕塑的真品还是现代的复制品？
同 genuine
反 phony

motive
/'məutiv/

n. 动机，目的
His motive was a wish to be helpful.
他的动机是想帮上点忙。
衍 motivation

summit
/'sʌmit/

n. 顶点；最高级会议
Fruitful negotiations on East-West tension can be achieved only at the summit. 只有举行最高级会议，缓和东西方紧张关系的谈判才能卓有成效。
同 peak
反 bottom
短语 summit conference 峰会

visible
/'vizəbl/

adj. 看得见的
He is visible only to his most intimate friends.
他只愿会见最熟悉的朋友。

飞跃词汇

provoke
/prə'vəuk/

vt. 激怒
In doing so, he has provoked general rage.
他这样做已引起了公愤。

interrogate
/in'terəgeit/

vt. 审问，询问
The policeman interrogated the witness about the accident. 警察询问目击者有关事故的情况。
衍 interrogation *n.*
同 question

provision
/prə'viʒən/

n. 供应;预备
They made provision for their children's education.
他们为孩子的教育预作安排。

provocative
/prə'vɔkətiv/

adj. 激起愤怒的;挑衅的
Her style is provocative of controversy.
她的风格很容易引起争议。
衍 provocation *n.*

UNIT 37

基础词汇

broad
/brɔːd/

adj. & n. 广泛的；宽的
He is tall and has broad shoulders.
他身高肩宽。
反 narrow

intimacy
/'intiməsi/

n. 亲密；亲昵行为
I like sharing these little intimacies.
我喜欢分享这种说点儿悄悄话的乐趣。
同 closeness
反 alienation

loosen
/'luːsn/

v. 解开
He didn't loosen his tie.
他没有松开领带。
短语 loosen up 使松弛

extend
/ik'stend/

v. 延伸；舒展（肢体）
He extends his hand in greeting.
他伸出手表示欢迎。
衍 extension n.

function
/'fʌŋkʃən/

n. 职能；功能
The function of a hammer is to hit nails into woods.
锤子的作用是把钉子敲进木头。
同 fundam

fundamentally
/ˌfʌndə'mentəli/

adv. 基础地，根本地
Fundamentally, he is a responsible man.
从根本上讲，他是个有责任心的人。
同 basically

guilty
/'gilti/

adj. 犯罪的；内疚的

He was found not guilty by reason of insanity.
他因为精神失常而被裁定无罪。

衍 guilt *n.*

同 remorseful

反 proud

搭配 be guilty of 有罪的，有过失的

hostile
/'hɔstail/

adj. & n. 敌对的

His colleagues were hostile to his suggestions.
他的同事们反对他的建议。

衍 hostility *n.*

同 aggressive

反 friendly

搭配 be hostile to 怀有敌意的

brow
/brau/

n. 眉毛；(面部)表情

His brow was sad.
他面露忧伤的表情。

lounge
/laundʒ/

n. 长沙发；休息室

He is waiting for you in the departure lounge.
他在候机室等你呢。

move
/muːv/

v. & n. 移动；步骤

Don't move your hand.
手别动。

短语 make one's move 采取行动

over
/'əuvə/

adv. & prep. 结束；在……之上

He lived over a bakery.
他住在一家面包店的楼上。

extensive
/ik'stensiv/

adj. 广泛的

He maintained extensive contacts with his former colleagues.

他与以前的同事保持着广泛的联系。

同 expansive

反 limited

overall
/ˌəuvər'ɔːl/

adj. 全部的，全面的

Overall, imports account for half of our stock.

总的来说，进口货占我们存货的一半。

pull
/pul/

v. 拉，拖

Don't pull my hair!

别扯我的头发！

短语　pull oneself together 重新振作起来

pull one's legs 开玩笑

expose
/ik'spəuz/

v. 使暴露；揭露

The skin will peal off your back if you expose it to too much sun. 如果你过多的晒太阳，背就会脱皮。

搭配　expose...to 使处于……作用(影响)

mourn
/mɔːn/

v. 哀悼

I shall always love Guy and mourn for him.

我将永远爱盖伊并悼念他。

同 lament

drag
/dræg/

v. & n. 拖

We dragged ourselves out of bed at the crack of dawn.

天刚破晓，我们就强迫自己起床了。

短语　drag on 拖延

crucial
/'kruːʃəl/

adj. 至关紧要的

He has to make a crucial decision.
他必须做出关键性的决定。

同 vital

搭配 be crucial to 对……很关键

pull through

vt. 渡过难关;恢复健康

No one thought the patient would pull through.
没人认为这个病人还能恢复健康。

suppose
/sə'pəuz/

v. 推想,假设

Let's suppose it to be so.
让我们假定情况是这样。

同 assume

supervise
/'sjuːpəvaiz/

v. 监督,管理

This professor supervised 5 postgraduate students.
这位教授指导了 5 名研究生。

衍 supervision *n.*

同 monitor

fall behind

落后(于)

He fell behind when we were climbing the mountain.
我们爬山时,他掉队了。

suppress
/sə'pres/

vt. 镇压;抑制

she was struggling to suppress her tears.
她拼命不让自己哭出声来。

turn out

生产;关掉

Please turn out the light.
请把灯关掉。

拓展词汇

提高词汇

Week 6 Day 2

draw up

草拟

I haven't yet drawn up vacation plans.
我尚未订出假期计划。

volume
/'vɔljuːm/

n. 卷,册;体积;音量

The music doubled in volume.
音乐的声音加大了一倍。

write off

注销,勾销

All the newspaper reporters wrote the play off as
useless. 所有的报纸记者都认为这出戏毫无意义。

automate
/'ɔːtəmeit/

v. 使自动化

It is a fully automated production line.
这是一条全自动生产线。

衍 automation *n.*

intricate
/'intrikit/

adj. 复杂的

A detective story usually has an intricate plot.
侦探小说通常有错综复杂的情节。

同 complex
反 simple

crew
/kruː/

n. 全体人员

The aircraft has a crew of four.
这架飞机有4名机组成员。

pry
/prai/

v. 探查;撬开

Please pry the tin open.
请把罐头撬开。

搭配 pry into 打听,刺探

255

superiority
/sjuːˌpiəri'ɔriti/

n. 优越

There is no doubt that the superiority of these goods to others is easy to see. 毫无疑问,这些货物与其他货物相比,其优越性是显而易见的。

衍 superior *adj.*

反 inferiority

搭配 be superior to 比······优越

---

drastic
/'dræstik/

adj. 猛烈的

The goverment takes a drastic step to fight against corruption.

政府采取严厉的步骤打击腐败。

同 radical

---

avail
/ə'veil/

v. 有益于

All our efforts availed us little.

我们徒劳无功。

短语 without avail 徒劳的

---

rotate
/rəu'teit/

v. (使)旋转

The earth rotates around the sun.

地球绕着太阳转。

衍 rotation *n.*

同 revolve

---

autonomy
/ɔː'tɔnəmi/

n. 自治

The autonomy of every individual should be respected.

每个人的人身自由应该受到尊重。

---

criterion
/krai'tiəriən/

n. 标准

A debater's highest criterion is reasoning.

衡量辩论家的最高准则是推论能力。

同 yardstick

飞跃词汇

supplement
/'sʌplimənt/

vt. 补充

He often has strawberry as a vitamin supplement.
他常常吃草莓来补充维生素。

同 add to

intriguing
/in'triːgiŋ/

adj. 引起兴趣(或好奇心)的

To me that's what is really intriguing about him.
对我来说,他让人感兴趣的地方即在于此。

同 fascinating

UNIT 38

exterior
/ik'stiəriə/

adj. 外部的

He is responsible for the exterior decoration of the building.他负责这栋楼的外部装修。

同 outward

反 interior

suspend
/sə'spend/

v. 暂停

Henry was suspended from school for a week for bad conduct. 亨利因行为不端被停学一周。

dreadful
/'dredfəl/

adj. 可怕的

The result would be dreadful for you.
结局对你将是很不愉快的。

average
/'ævəridʒ/

n. & adj. 平均数;普通的

The boy's work at school is above average.
这个男孩的学习成绩属于中上水平。

短语 on average 平均

routine
/ruː'tiːn/

n. 日常事务

Despite these problems,routine work is continuing.
尽管有这些问题,日常工作还是照常进行。

drip
/drip/

v. (使)滴下

The rain dripped from the trees.
雨水从树上滴下。

external
/ik'stə:nl/

adj. 外部的

The external features of the building are very attractive.
那建筑物的外观非常漂亮。

同 exterior

反 internal

---

gymnasium
/dʒim'neiziəm/

n. 健身房,体育馆

Doing exercises in the gymnasium is good for health.
在健身房做运动对健康有益。

---

loyalty
/'lɔiəlti/

n. 忠诚,忠心

Everyone is supposed to have family loyalties.
每个人都应有忠于家庭的感情。

衍 loyal *adj.*

同 faithfulness

反 faithlessness

搭配 show loyalty to 忠诚于

---

avoid
/ə'vɔid/

vt. 避免

You should avoid being late for your class.
你应该避免上课迟到。

搭配 avoid doing 避开,避免

---

surprisingly
/sə'praiziŋli/

adv. 令人惊讶地

Surprisingly , she won the first prize.
令人吃惊的是,她得了第一名。

衍 surprised *adj.*

---

luck
/lʌk/

n. 运气

My luck is in.
我的运道很好。

短语 try one's luck 碰碰运气

259

much
/mʌtʃ/

adj. & adv. **许多的，大量的**

There isn`t much coal left.

剩下的煤不多了。

搭配　make much of 很重视，强调

extent
/ik'stent/

n. **范围**

He saw the full extent of the lake from the air.

他从空中看到了那个湖的全景。

搭配　to a certian extent 在某种程度上

survive
/sə'vaiv/

v. **幸存**

Only two people survived the fire.

这场大火中只有两个人幸免于难。

衍　survival *n.*

反　cease, die

rough
/rʌf/

adj. **粗糙的**

What rough luck!

真倒霉！

短语　in the rough 粗略的，大致的

available
/ə'veiləbl/

adj. **可利用的**

All the available money has been used.

手头所有的钱都用完了。

同　accessible

intuition
/ˌintju(ː)'iʃən/

n. **直觉**

Everyone has the power of intuition.

每个人都有直觉。

同　instinct

crude
/kru:d/

adj. 天然的,未加工的;粗鲁的

America can not have a crude interference in another country's internal affairs. 美国不能对别国内政进行粗暴干涉。

同 coarse

反 refined

furious
/'fjuəriəs/

adj. 狂怒的

He was furious to hear about it.
他听到这件事勃然大怒。

同 angry

反 pleased

搭配 be furious with sb. 暴怒

furnish
/'fə:niʃ/

v. 提供;装备

The records furnished the information required.
纪录提供所需资料。

同 supply

multiply
/'mʌltiplai/

v. 繁殖;增加

Fear multiplies the difficulties of life.
恐惧会使生活变得更加困难。

同 increase

budget
/'bʌdʒit/

n. 预算

The Finance Minister will introduce a new budget in April. 财政大臣将于四月提出新预算方案。

短语 on a budget 精打细算

pump
/pʌmp/

n. & vt. 泵;抽吸

The heart pumps blood into the veins.
心脏把血液压送至血管。

261

拓展词汇

surge
/səːdʒ/

v. 汹涌澎湃
As soon as the valve was opened, the water surged in.
阀门一开,水就涌进去了。
同 swell
反 pacify

punctual
/ˈpʌŋktʃuəl/

adj. 准时的
She's never punctual in answering letters.
她从不及时回信。
同 on time
反 late

surpass
/səˈpɑːs/

vt. 超越
His work surpassed expectations.
他的工作比预期的好。
同 exceed

figure out

计算出
Please help me to figure out the sums.
请帮我把这些数目算出来。

提高词汇

bully
/ˈbuli/

v. 威吓,威逼
I wanted to tell you everything but he bullied me out of it. 我想把一切都告诉你,但他吓唬我不要讲。
同 intimidate

overlap
/ˌəuvəˈlæp/

v. (与……)交迭
The two theories overlap on one important point.
这两种理论在关键的一点上相同。

提高词汇

hurl
/həːl/

vt. 愤慨地说

He hurled insults at the driver who almost crashed into him. 他把那个几乎撞着他的司机臭骂了一顿。

drawback
/'drɔːbæk/

n. 缺点

The main drawback to this product is that it is too sour.
这个产品的主要缺点是太酸。

同 disadvantage

反 advantage

辨析　drawback 缺点，不足之处
　　　defect 缺陷，短处

intrinsic
/in'trinsik/

adj. 固有的，内在的

The necklace was made of glass, so it had little intrinsic worth. 这个项链是玻璃的，所以本身并不值钱。

同 innate

反 extrinsic

twist
/twist/

v. 扭曲

Twist the handle to the right and the box will open.
将手柄向右转，箱子就会开了。

短语　twist and turn 蜿蜒

crumble
/'krʌmbl/

v. & n. 弄碎，粉碎

The quake crumbled the walls of the hospital.
地震把那所医院的墙震塌了。

同 break apart

vigorous
/'vigərəs/

adj. 精力旺盛的

Taking exercises can keep people vigorous.
锻炼身体可以保持体力旺盛。

同 energetic

反 feeble

263

punch
/pʌntʃ/

v. 以拳重击
He punched the man on the nose.
他对着那人的鼻子猛击一拳。
短语　punch out 记录下班时间

invariable
/in'veəriəbl/

adj. 不变地
It's his invariable habit to take a nap.
睡午觉是他的老习惯。
同　unchanging
反　changeable

overhear
/ˌəuvə'hiə/

vt. 无意中听到;偷听
I wouldn' t like to be overheard.
我不想有人听到我的话。

cruise
/kruːz/

vi. & n. 巡游,巡航
We cruised to Qingdao on vacation.
我们航游到青海去度假。
同　sail

UNIT 39

基础词汇

furniture
/'fə:nitʃə/

n. 家具
A set of new furniture is needed.
需要一套新家具。

curious
/'kjuəriəs/

adj. 好奇的,求知的
Children are curious about everything.
儿童对什么都感到好奇。

衍 curiosity *n.*

同 interested

反 indifferent

搭配 be curious about 好奇的

dumb
/dʌm/

adj. 哑的
She was born dumb.
她生来就是哑巴。

同 mute

短语 play dumb 装聋作哑

award
/ə'wɔ:d/

n. & vt. 奖品;授予
The university awarded him an honorary degree.
这所大学授给他名誉学位。

crush
/krʌʃ/

vt. 压碎,(使)起皱
Her dresses were badly crushed when she took them out of the suitcase. 她把衣服从衣箱里拿出来时,衣服被压得一塌糊涂。

同 squash

短语 crush out 榨出,挤出

Week 6 Day 4

extra
/'ekstrə/

adj. & n. 额外的

At this hotel a hot bath is an extra.
在这家旅馆洗澡要另外收费的。

further
/'fəːðə/

adj. 更远的, 深一层的

Do you have any further questions to ask?
你还有什么问题要问吗?

hurt
/həːt/

v. & n. 刺痛, 伤害

I fell off my bicycle and hurt my arm.
我从自行车上摔下来, 摔伤了胳膊。

同 injure

involve
/in'vɔlv/

vt. 包括; 笼罩

Fog involved the village.
迷雾笼罩着村庄。

短语 be involved in 参与; 卷入(事件中)

investigate
/in'vestigeit/

v. 调查, 研究

Scientists investigate nature to learn more about it.
为了更多地了解自然界, 科学家对它进行调查研究。

衍 investigation *n.*

同 look into

burst
/bəːst/

v. 爆裂, 爆破

He burst free from the chains.
他挣脱锁链获得了自由。

短语 burst into 闯入

pursue
/pə'sjuː/

vt. 追求

Women's freedom to pursue careers are liberated from bearing children. 妇女从育儿中解脱出来, 有了追求职业生涯的自由。

衍 pursuit *n.*

同 chase

266

基础词汇

拓展词汇

Week 6 Day 4

push
/pʊʃ/

vt. **推动;逼迫**

She pushed herself to her feet.
她费劲地站了起来。

短语　push... aside 把……搁置一边

drive
/draiv/

v. **推动,发动**

The urge to survive drives them on.
求生的欲望驱使他们继续努力。

搭配　drive at 朝……努力

pain
/pein/

n. **痛苦**

A cut gives pain.
割伤引起疼痛。

辨析　pain 疼痛,苦痛
　　　hurt 伤害
　　　sore 痛处,溃疡

短语　at pains 尽心,费尽苦心

call
/kɔːl/

n. & v. **喊叫;打电话**

Will you please call me a taxi?
请你给我叫一辆出租汽车好吗?

同　summon

短语　call on 拜访

swift
/swift/

adj. **快的,敏捷的**

The river is too swift to swim.
这河水流太急,不能游泳。

同　speedy
反　slow

awake
/ə'weik/

v. & adj. **醒着的;叫醒**

We awake next morning to a fine drizzle.
第二天早晨我们醒来时天在下着蒙蒙细雨。

but for

要不是

But for the doctor's skill, he would have died.
要不是医生医术高明,他早就死了。

suspicious
/sə'spiʃəs/

adj. 可疑的;怀疑的

I am a bit suspicious about the box left in the corridor.
我对放在走廊里的盒子起了疑心。

衍 suspicion *n.*

同 skeptical

搭配 feel suspicious of（about）起疑心

get along with

和睦相处

He doesn't get along with anybody in the office.
他和办公室里其他人都处得不好。

due to

由于;应归于

The discovery of the law is due to Newton.
这条定律是由牛顿发现的。

overlook
/ˌəuvə'luk/

vt. 俯瞰;忽略

They overlooked the enormous risks involved.
他们忽略了其中牵涉的极大危险。

同 neglect

overwhelm
/ˌəuvə'welm/

vt. 压倒

I was overwhelmed by their kindness and moved to tears. 我被善良的他们感动地落泪了。

ruin
/ruin/

v. & n. (使)堕落;毁灭

The news meant the ruin of all our hopes.
这消息使我们的所有希望都破灭了。

同 destruction

短语 in ruins 成废墟

make for

向……前进

The ship made for the open sea.
该船向公海驶去。

ironically
/ɑiˈrɔnikli/

adv. 讽刺地
He smiled ironically.
他微笑中带有讽刺意味。
同 sarcastically

sake
/seik/

n. 缘故
For my own sake as well as for yours, I will do my very best. 为了我自己也是为了你，我将尽我的全力去做。
搭配 for the sake of 为了

extinct
/ikˈstiŋkt/

adj. 熄灭的；灭绝的
All hope was extinct.
所有希望都落空了。
衍 extinction *n.*
同 nonexistent
反 existing

cumulative
/ˈkjuːmjulətiv/

adj. 累积的
The cumulative effects of many illnesses made him a weak man. 多种疾病长期的折磨使他身体虚弱。

lump
/lʌmp/

n. 小块
Do you put one lump or two in my coffee?
你在我的咖啡里放一块还是两块方糖？

murmur
/ˈməːmə/

n. & v. 低沉连续的声音；低声说
The breeze murmured in the pines.
松林里微风沙沙作响。

swerve
/swəːv/

v. 突然转向
A dog ran in front of the car and we swerved to aviod it. 一只狗跑到汽车前面，我们急转弯避开了它。

extinguish
/ik'stiŋgwiʃ/

vt. 熄灭

Hope of his safe arrival slowly extinguished.
对他平安到达的希望慢慢破灭了。

同 quench
反 ignite

curb
/kɜːb/

n. 抑制

The government makes ease curbs on freedom of speech and assembly. 政府放宽了对言论与聚会自由的限制。

搭配 place a curb on 限制

swell
/swel/

v. (使)膨胀,增大

The sails swelled out in the wind.船帆在风中鼓起。

同 bulge

luminous
/'luːminəs/

adj. 发光的

The sun and stars are luminous bodies.
太阳和恒星是发光体。

同 radiant
反 dim

sustain
/sə'stein/

vt. 支撑

An unshakable faith sustained me.
一种不可动摇的信念支持着我。

multitude
/'mʌltitjuːd/

n. 多数,大批

A great multitude gathered in the street.
街道上聚集了一大群人。

同 mass
搭配 a multitude of 许多

tycoon
/tai'kuːn/

n. 企业界大亨

He is an oil tycoon.
他是石油巨头。

UNIT 40

awareness
/ə'weənis/

n. 意识

A good senator must have an awareness of what common people really want. 一个好的参议员必须明白普通老百姓真正需要什么。

同 consciousness

---

put across

使……了解，接受

A good commercial puts across the attractive features of a product. 好广告能突显产品吸引人的特征。

---

switch
/switʃ/

n. 开关

Please turn off the switch.
请把开关关掉。

---

dust
/dʌst/

n. 灰尘

There was half an inch of dust on the books.
书本上有半英寸厚的灰尘。

短语 as dry as dust 枯燥无味的

---

fuse
/fjuːz/

v. 熔合

He helped the old party fuse with the new one.
他促使旧党和新党合并。

---

isolate
/'aisəleit/

vt. 使隔离

People with contagious diseases should be isolated.
传染病患者应予以隔离。

衍 isolation *n.*

同 seclude

extremely
/ik'striːmli/

adv. 极端地,非常地

I enjoyed the play extremely.
我非常欣赏那出戏。

衍 extreme *n.*

mute
/mjuːt/

v. & a. 哑的;减弱

They spoke in muted voices.
他们轻声说话。

owe
/əu/

v. 欠(债等);把……归功于

We owe our parents a lot.
我们亏欠父母的实在太多了。

搭配 owe...to 把……归功于

symbol
/'simbəl/

n. 符号;象征

The lion is a symbol of courage.
狮子是勇武的象征。

衍 symbolic *adj.*

同 token

dynamic
/dai'næmik/

adj. 精力充沛的;动力的

I need a dynamic loudspeaker.
我需要一个电动扬声器。

同 energetic

反 lifeless

eye
/ai/

n. 眼睛;视力

His eyes were shining.
他的双目炯炯有神。

短语 have one's eye on 密切注意

rush
/rʌʃ/

v. 冲奔;涌现

The rain rushed against the house.
暴雨冲打屋子。

短语 in a rush 急急忙忙

基础词汇

puzzle
/'pʌzl/

n. & v. 难题;迷惑
Lucy looked a little puzzled.
露西看上去有点儿困惑。
同 confuse

at random

胡乱地,随便地
Don't answer at random, think first.
别乱回答,先想一想。
同 haphazard

拓展词汇

visit
/'vizit/

n. & vt. 拜访,访问
When we were in London, we visited the Tower twice.
我们在伦敦期间两次游览了伦敦塔。

symptom
/'simptəm/

n. 症状
Call your doctor for advice if the symptoms persist for more than a week. 如果症状持续一周以上就要征求医生的意见了。
同 syndrome

cynical
/'sinikəl/

adj. 愤世嫉俗的
He was getting harder and more cynical about life.
他变得更加冷酷和愤世嫉俗。
同 pessimistic
反 optimistic

Week 6 Day 5

awkward
/'ɔːkwəd/

adj. 笨拙的
An awkward girl is no help in the kitchen.
一个笨手笨脚的女孩在厨房里帮不了忙。
同 unskillful
反 adroit

own up to

承认
You had better own up to your faults.
你最好承认你的错误。

extract
/ik'strækt/

n. & vt. 摘录；榨取

Dealers, sometimes encouraged by their firms, would go to great lengths to extract information from employees of rival firms. 经销商有时受公司怂恿，会竭尽全力从对手公司员工那里套取情报。

衍 extraction n.

搭配 extract ... from 提取，提炼

by far

到目前为止

It will be by far the most urgent issue of the age.
显然，这将是当代最紧迫的问题。

lure
/luə/

vt. 引诱

Lured by the lust of gold, the pioneers pushed onward.
开拓者在黄金的诱惑下奋力前进。

同 entice

irritate
/'iriteit/

vt. 激怒；刺激

The smoke irritated my eyes.
烟熏得我眼睛怪难受的。

衍 irritation n.

同 enrage

put away

储存……备用

She put her clothes away in the dresser.
她把衣服收放在衣橱里。

run over

辗过

The bus ran over his legs.
公共汽车辗过他的双腿。

cut down

减少

We must cut our expenses down somehow.
我们得设法减少开支。

sympathy
/'simpəθi/

n. 同情，同情心

These people need our help and sympathy.
这些人需要我们的帮助和同情。

衍 sympathetic *adj.*

搭配 show sympathy for 同情

---

buzz
/bʌz/

v. 嗡嗡声

The phone buzzed.
电话发出嗡嗡的声音。

---

duplicate
/'djuːplikeit/

adj. & n. 复制的；复制品

If you have lost your key, I can give you a duplicate.
你如果把钥匙丢了，我可以另外给你一把。

衍 duplication *n.*

同 copy

反 original

---

dwell
/dwel/

vi. 居住

They dwell in the middle of the forest.
他们住在林子里。

同 live

搭配 dwell on 细想（详述，详论）

---

luxury
/'lʌkʃəri/

n. 奢侈，华贵

She has accustomed to luxury.
她习惯于奢侈的享受。

衍 luxurious *adj.*

---

current
/'kʌrənt/

adj. & n. 当前的；(思想的)动向

Newspapers influence the current of public opinion.
报纸影响舆论的倾向。

swing
/swiŋ/

v. 摇摆,摆动
The door swung open.门打开了。
短语 in full swing 正处于全盛时期

typical
/'tipikəl/

adj. 典型的
This is typical of you ! 那只有你才干得出来!
同 characteristic
搭配 be typical of 特有的,独特的

mount
/maunt/

v. 增长
Production costs are steadily mounting.
生产成本在不断增加。
同 increase
反 decrease

mystical
/'mistikəl/

adj. 神秘的
The mystical food of the sacrament is mysterious.
圣餐的灵食具有神秘色彩。
同 mysterious

extravagant
/ik'strævəgənt/

adj. 奢侈的
He leads a kind of extravagant life.他过着奢侈的生活。
衍 extravagance *n.*
同 lavish
反 thrifty

curriculum
/kə'rikjuləm/

n. 课程
The curriculum in engineering is difficult.
工科课程很难。

subscribe
/səb'skraib/

vi. 订阅
He subscribes to *China Daily*.
他订阅《中国日报》。
搭配 subscribe to 订阅

Index

Index

Index

Index

Index

Index